ZAR

I've been writing stories for just about as long as I've been reading them – it's rumoured that I'm related to Elizabeth Gaskell, so maybe it's in the genes!

I live in a country cottage in the UK with a naughty mouse catching, curtain climbing cat, my wonderful guitar playing, video making, Minecraft mad teenage son and a wine drinking, sun loving, master chef in the making, sexy alpha hero.

I love my family, sexy high heels, sunshine, wine, good food, cats, horses, dogs, music, coffee, writing and reading - but not necessarily in that order! And I like my heroes just how I like my coffee – hot, strong and moreish.

You can find more about me, and all my contact details at www.zarastoneley.com. Please stop by – I love to meet new people

# Summer of Surrender

## ZARA STONELEY

HarperImpulse an imprint of
HarperCollinsPublishers Ltd
77–85 Fulham Palace Road
Hammersmith, London W6 8JB

www.harpercollins.co.uk

A Paperback Original 2014

First published in Great Britain in ebook format by HarperImpulse 2013

Copyright © Zara Stoneley 2013

Cover Images © Shutterstock.com

Zara Stoneley asserts the moral right to
be identified as the author of this work

A catalogue record for this book
is available from the British Library

ISBN: 978-0-00-758488-8

This novel is entirely a work of fiction.
The names, characters and incidents portrayed in it are
the work of the author's imagination. Any resemblance to
actual persons, living or dead, events or localities is
entirely coincidental.

Automatically produced by Atomik ePublisher from Easypress

*To my family, who have always encouraged me to follow my dreams, and my very own sexy hero who has provided the inspiration and support to turn them into reality.*

# Chapter 1

'Shit.' Whoever said climbing gates in a maxi dress was possible had got it wrong. Seriously wrong. Or maybe no one had been stupid enough to say it.

Kezia Martin clung on to the top of the wobbling timber and considered her options. Rolling off was a definite possibility, except that the driveway looked like it had a high 'ouch' factor. Although she was a million miles from sophisticated, even she knew that a gravelled face was not a good look. But there didn't seem to be an option B. Apart from the 'split your dress at the seams' one, and she did actually like this dress quite a lot. And as it made up fifty per cent of her going-out wardrobe, she wasn't ready to sacrifice it, and neither did she want expose her thighs – or worse – to the world.

Not that there was much of the world here to see anyway. The monosyllabic taxi driver had dropped her off by a five-bar gate in the middle of nowhere, and scarpered before she had the chance to say she'd changed her mind. Not that she really wanted to face another trip in his car.

She'd actually been feeling pretty positive, if knackered, when she'd staggered out of the train station. And even the one battered taxi that was parked in the otherwise deserted rank didn't deflate her too much. The driver had taken her bag without a great deal of enthusiasm, shoved his newspaper onto the passenger seat and raised an eyebrow when she'd read out the address, which seemed a bit rude. He'd muttered something that she could have sworn sounded like 'you don't look like one of them,' but she could have got that bit wrong. Then he'd stoically ignored her and driven further and further into the countryside before unceremoniously dumping her, grabbing his fare and driving off in his belching car. Which was doubly rude.

She would have been more worried, but the back of beyond was probably a good place to be right now. A good place to start again. And anyway, she was too darned tired to really think about anything, apart from the comfy bed that just had to be waiting for her. It had to be.

Or maybe not. There wasn't an intercom, not even a bell, just the gate, firmly fastened with a chain that wouldn't have looked out of place attached to an anchor. She'd tried hollering and she'd tried waiting, though not for that long since patience wasn't her greatest virtue. Then she'd decided that there obviously wasn't a guard dog, and she was too tired to sit in the road any longer. At least on the other side she might find somewhere to sit down and wait. It had to be better than staying on the outside. So she'd thrown her rucksack and guitar over the gate and planned on following them. Which involved hitching up the dress to just over her knees and taking advantage of the generous slit down one side. The problem was there was no slit on the other side, so once she was astride the gate, things got tricky. Whichever way she tried to move there was the tell-tale sound of the snapping of stitches. Bugger.

She would ring for help, but her mobile was in her rucksack. On the ground, right where she was heading. Which left two options: praying to God for help, or making an even bigger fool of herself. She shut her eyes, which always helped with thinking. And praying.

'What-' there was a God, with a wicked sense of humour seeing as she just about fell off the precarious perch, '-are you doing?'

Well, maybe not a God. She turned as far as she could, cricking her neck in the process, and could just about make out a tall, lean figure. The low sun behind him made everything but his outline pretty much indiscernible, so she screwed up her eyes to try and focus on him. Which didn't help.

'Are you going to give me a hand, or just stand there?'

'No to the first, yes to the second.' He didn't just stand there, though. He took a couple of steps nearer, so that she could make out quite clearly that this wasn't some mysterious God, just a mysterious mortal. With a soft voice, which had an undertone that was making her skin prickle.

'Very helpful, *not*.' It was muttered under her breath, but she had the distinct feeling, from the look on his face, that he'd heard. Kezia didn't believe in love at first sight, or hate either. But right now this guy was making her think that the second was maybe an option. He stood, arms folded, feet astride and just looked through narrowed eyes while she clung to his gate. Well, she assumed it was his gate, seeing as he was on the other side.

Black t-shirt, black pasted-on jeans, black hair, black face. Or at least a not-very-pleased face. Inscrutable was probably the word, inscrutable in quite a brooding way, which made her feel even more of a dishevelled mess.

'This is private property.' His tone was mild, but he was obviously used to people taking notice of it. Which riled her. She'd been invited here, for fuck's sake.

'What do you think I am? Stupid? I did actually realise that, for a start the bloody big padlock's a bit of a giveaway. But, I was told to come here, today, by Marie.' *And I feel bloody silly having a conversation while I'm wobbling on a gate.* 'You know? Marie, who runs the place?' Okay, sarcasm was the lowest form of wit, but right now it worked for her.

'We're shut.'

'Well that's bloody obvious by the mega-duty chain. But I. Have. Got. An. Appointment.' She spoke slowly, hoping it would help.

'Sorry, there are no appointments until September.' He took a step back, arms still folded across his body and looked like he was about to go.

'You have got to be joking!' Kezia couldn't believe it. He stood there and replied, calmly 'we're shut'. Just like you would say a shop is shut. And she'd just travelled over a thousand bloody miles for this! He didn't look like the kidding type, though. Closer up he looked like the strong, silent, 'I'm sexy and I know it' type. Except the corner of his mouth had tipped slightly into a shape that looked vaguely promising; almost a smile. All she had to do was work out how to humour him, and still get in. 'You can't be shut, buster. I might not be sure I want to be here and you sure as hell don't look like you want me to be. But I am. And I'm going to do this if it kills us both. So do me a favour and either help me down or shut your eyes, because me climbing over isn't going to be a pretty sight.'

'Is that your stuff?' He nodded his head towards her well-worn rucksack and battered guitar case.

She nodded. Two long strides and he'd laid his hand on the guitar case, and she just knew what he was going to do. Throw it back over, and then probably her with it. 'Don't you dare.' Nobody touched her guitar. The rucksack, yeah, but not the guitar. She made a grab to stop him, forgetting she needed to hang on, heard the unmistakeable sound of tearing fabric and fell. Shit, torn dress and face. Shit, shit, shit. Except she didn't hit the ground.

How anyone could move that fast she didn't know. But his warm hands were on her waist, which meant her feet hit the ground before her body. 'Oo.' She was inches from him, and his hands were still on her body and it didn't feel like any touch she could remember. It was a lulling touch, a warmth that held a kind of promise that she didn't quite recognise.

And she still had her mouth open. She snapped it shut. He let go, in his own time, but didn't move away.

'Are you okay?'

4

She nodded. Her tongue didn't work. It was stuck to the roof of her mouth because this man was pure unadulterated sex. He was surrounded by an aura that was screaming out 'touch me, want me.' She reached out tentatively without thinking. And then he moved. One step away. Out of arms' reach.

'I'm…' Well, she was red hot for one. All over. The first flush was down to the way he held her, the second was please-earth-swallow-me-up embarrassment.

'You are?'

'I'm Kezia Martin, how do you do? I do have an appointment, and please don't throw me back over the gate. You see I talked to Maria when we were in Capri and she said that if I came here now, well as soon as I'd finished in Italy, which she knew was two days ago, she said she'd be able to—'

He held up a hand. 'Whoa. Do you always go at that speed? Slow down, you're giving me a headache.'

She was babbling, she knew she was babbling. It was a bad habit she had when she felt stupid or embarrassed. She would always talk too much to cover for herself.

'So…' He paused. Studying her with eyes that appeared black in the dimming light, he looked her over with a lazy smile that brought out a rash of goose bumps over her arms. No, it couldn't be his smile; smiles didn't do that. It had to be the fact that it was getting cooler. She wrapped her arms across her chest and tried to ignore the prickle of her nipples through the fine silk of her dress. His gaze drifted briefly over her body and she shivered involuntarily. Her hair had to be a mess, her dress had a rip somewhere – she wasn't quite sure where yet, and she daren't look. Her body was on full alert, as though any moment now she expected him to pounce.

'You're cold.'

*If it's the nipples you've spotted, that's nothing to do with the temperature.* 'I'm fine.' There was a slight tremble in the words and she swallowed, trying to clear her throat, get back to normality and break the spell that he'd woven.

He ignored the words. Looked her over slowly again and seemed to come to an abrupt decision.

'Seeing as you seem to be on the wrong side of the gate now…' He paused. *Wrong side, right side, depends on whose saying the words, mate.* 'You might as well come and explain in the house.' He picked her rucksack up, swung it over one shoulder as though it was feather-light (which she knew for a fact it wasn't as she'd hauled it across half of Europe, frequently cursing the fact that it was crammed full with most of her worldly goods) and she made a grab for her guitar, which he seemed to know was off limits. Then he walked off with an effortless stride that ate up the ground silently.

She felt like a dog scampering after him, trying to keep up, across a yard she barely had time to take in, except for the fact that it had to be the cleanest yard she'd ever seen. Down a path between immaculate flowerbeds that led to a slightly faded, but obviously once-imposing, farmhouse.

He slowed briefly, to push the large oak door open wider, and had marched across the worn flagstones, dropped the rucksack and was pouring coffee before she'd even had chance to get her bearings. Or catch her breath.

'So?' He passed her a mug, then placed his own on the table between them and waited. For an explanation. She opened her mouth, then closed it. Thing was, why did she have to explain at all? He obviously lived here, and he obviously, from his reaction, knew Marie. But now she had her hands wrapped around a warm mug and her heart rate had returned to normal she was beginning to feel that hate, well, dislike, again. Who did he think he was? At least at this distance, with a table between them, the intensity had dwindled to a gentle simmer.

'I run the business with Dan and Marie.'

Ah, he was a mind-reader. His long, slim finger stroked around the rim of the mug. She took a moment to look at him properly.

He was lean, toned rather than muscled-up, and every part of him seemed to be essential, nothing wasted, nothing extra. His arms were defined, as an artist would define their model. He seemed to possess a quiet strength, holding back, contained and yet on the edge, as though a single command could unleash his power. His hair was dark to the point of black, as were his eyes – it hadn't been a trick of the failing light, even here under the artificial glare there was an almost unnatural depth to the colour. His features were aquiline. Enigmatic, hidden. She felt that shudder again and decided to stop examining him so closely.

'Marie offered me a job.' She took a sip, concentrating on the steam rising from the liquid. 'So, I'm here.'

'And she's not.' His voice was gentle, as though he didn't want to frighten her.

'She's not?'

'Nope.' He leaned back, and she was aware of him stretching his legs out under the table, closer to her own. She crossed her ankles under the chair, scrunching up into a smaller space.

He smiled. 'Marie and Dan are away, everyone is away. I'm here looking after the horses, and we're shut for the summer, so I'm afraid there isn't a job.'

'But, she said, she promised.' Kezia reached for her rucksack. She needed this job, needed money, more to the point. She was stuck here in the middle of nowhere, down to her last few pounds and with nowhere else to go. 'Look, I'll ring her if you don't believe me.' When she could find her phone, why the hell could she never find things? It was in the side pocket, it was always…. No, it was in the top.

'Don't worry. Leave it. You can stay here tonight and then in the morning…'

'No, I'm staying here. You've got to give me a job.'

His eyes narrowed a touch. *Ignore it*. 'Marie promised. Here.' She grabbed at her phone triumphantly and pulled up the list of contacts.

His hand came down over hers before she could search.

'I said, leave it.' The voice was still as soft, but there was that edge again. The edge that made her stomach clench with strange anticipation. She dragged her fingers away from the heat of his touch. Put her hands under the table.

'No.' Whatever spell he was used to casting over women, it wasn't going to work on her. She'd met loads of weirdos over the years; you always did when you led the nomadic kind of lifestyle her family had enjoyed. Not that 'enjoyed' was always the most appropriate word. But she'd learned how to deal with them. Look them in the eye, be firm. Or if that failed, you keep your eyes down and scarper.

'Yes.' His tone was even, firm, his gaze met hers and it was her that broke the contact first, looking down to stare into the murky depths of her coffee. 'You're tired. I'll show you to one of the guest rooms and we'll sort this in the morning. I'll talk to Marie, work out what we owe you.'

'I don't want to be owed something, I want a job.' She needed a job. This was supposed to be the start of a new life, of moving on. She was on her own now, and the time for crying was over. Now she was going to take control of her life, make something of herself. Stop running. Achieve something she could be proud of. And it was meant to start here. It was meant to start now.

When she'd met Marie at the yoga retreat in Italy, something had immediately drawn her to the older woman. Marie might have been the rich client, and she, Kezia, might have been tasked with the most menial jobs, but there was some recognition between the two women. A recognition of something shared that made them stop and talk, something that told Kezia it was okay to unburden herself. She'd told Marie things she'd never told anyone about her life, things that she never imagined she could trust a stranger with, but she'd known she wouldn't be judged by her. And before Marie left she gave Kezia her details, making her promise to come to England when her work ran out at the start of the summer and the Italians went away. She assured her that there would be a job, a place she could settle in. A future.

Kezia suddenly realised that he had picked up her bag and was walking towards the staircase. She followed, suddenly tired. Tomorrow she'd feel better. Tomorrow the jetlag would be gone, along with the desperate feeling of loneliness, and she'd give this guy hell. *Give her what she was owed*, sod that.

He pushed open a door, grinning a teasing grin that made her heart jump. 'I'm James, by the way.' And then he was gone so quickly she wondered if she had imagined him even being in the room.

She sat down on the bed. Bounced once or twice. Comfy. Not like some of the beds she'd slept in over the last few years. The curtains were drawn, but she went over to the window and pulled them open, dimly making out the outlines of trees, fences, the ghostly shadow-like horses on the horizon. Maybe the middle of nowhere was a good place for her to be right now. Well, it would be perfect if it wasn't for him. Why did there always have to be someone intent on spoiling things?

Her fingers were drawn to the battered guitar case and she hesitated for a moment before unzipping it, pulling out the instrument and running her fingers over the polished wood. The one thing of any value that she had, the one thing that had the power to nourish her soul. The one constant left in her life, her companion. The corners of her mouth twitched, she sounded like a soppy, sorry-for-herself idiot. A good job it was all in her head and not out loud for macho-man James to hear.

She perched on the corner of the bed, then slowly started plucking at the strings, watching her reflection in the dressing-table mirror as her fingers moved. She did look a mess. He must have thought she was a right drop-out. Which she was in a way. She'd been called hippy chick, weirdo, gyppo and worse in her time. That's what being brought up by parents with different attitudes and beliefs did to your reputation. But she did miss them. And she missed Simon, even though she knew she had to leave him.

Was it only yesterday that she'd been in his arms? Yesterday when he'd cupped her face in his hands. 'You're leaving aren't you?'

She'd nodded.

'Why? We're okay.'

Yeah, okay. Just okay. And they were, they fitted easily together. He held her when she needed him to, kissed her gently when he wanted to make love, took her with an infinite care that made her heart ache.

They'd made love just before she'd left for the airport. Deep inside she knew he was hoping she'd change her mind, that *he* could change her mind. But neither of them said it. And deep inside she knew that it was time to say goodbye, to move on, that changing her mind would be a mistake she wasn't prepared to make. They'd lain naked on an old soft blanket that he always had in the back of the car, under the shade of a tree so that the warmth of the air bathed them, not the heat of the sun.

'I love you, Kez.' His blue gaze locked with hers. Trusting, open honest.

She linked her fingers through his. 'I love you too, Simon.' And she did. In her own way. The way that said she trusted him, she liked to be in his arms, he made her laugh….

'You don't have to go, or I can come with you.'

And the burning tears caught at the back of her throat as his soft, full lips took hers. He always made love to her gently, almost reverentially, but this time there had been an edge of desperation, too, and it made her sadder than any tears or pleas could have done.

She'd held him as he kissed her neck, cradled his head as his mouth had taken her nipple, teasing until her body started a gentle buzz. He'd burned a damp trail down her stomach with his tongue and then he'd sought out her nub, flicking it gently until lazy desire edged its way into her limbs and just as she'd teetered on the edge, just as the cry got caught in her throat he'd covered her body with his and thrust inside. They'd rocked together, their

10

bodies perfectly matched, their rhythm a well-practised beat and each time he pushed deep inside she'd felt sadder. She'd wrapped her legs around him as the ache inside grew, pulling him deeper until she could feel his balls against her. She desperately wanted to bury him so far inside that he'd reach the bit of her that needed more. She'd tangled her fingers in his hair as he'd gazed at her. And his mouth had covered hers and as the feeling grew to that unbearable point, he'd sucked gently on her tongue, drew it into his own mouth and she could smell his desire, taste his pain as they came together. Her body quivered around his, clinging desperately to every last inch, every last drop. Then, still entwined, he'd dropped his head on her shoulder and closed his eyes. And all she could think was she didn't have to go, didn't have to change everything. But she did. She had to sort herself out, become the person she knew she could be. Not the one that her past had forced her to become.

Kezia put the guitar gently down in the corner of the room, opened the curtains even wider so that the view would be there when she woke in the morning, and pulled the dress over her head.

The damage wasn't as bad as she'd expected. She had a slit up the other side now. Granted, not quite straight, but it stopped short of her knicker elastic. Which was good. It had pulled open at the seam, fraying the fabric, with one small jagged tear, but she could probably mend it. The green-blue fabric shimmered as she laid it over the back of the chair and she shoved her espadrilles underneath. The top sheet of the bed was crisp and fresh under her fingertips as she dragged it back, then rummaged in her rucksack for a t-shirt.

She was pooped. Well and truly done in. Tired from the journey, and that edge of uncertainty when you don't know where you were going and who you are going to meet. It could be good, she was used to it, but since her parents had gone it had been harder. There was nothing to comfort her at the end of the day. Well, there had been Simon, but she'd fucked that one up hadn't she?

But she had needed to. It was right to move on, it had to be. Exhaustion hit her as she lay back, pulled the cool cotton sheet up to her chin and closed her eyes. All she had to do was think of Simon, imagine him holding her and everything would be fine. But it was a dark, enigmatic stranger that jumped into her head, two black eyes burning into her as though he could read every thought.

'No.' She growled and rolled onto her stomach, burying her head under her arms. She really, really did not want to think about him anymore. He was a domineering, bossy know-it-all who thought he could dismiss her with a wave of his hand.

She could still feel the warmth of his skin burning through her dress. She screwed up her eyes. No, no, no. She did not, definitely, one hundred per cent did not want to think about that. He'd held her for two seconds flat, then jumped away before she could make the mistake of touching him back. Bastard. What made him think he could touch her, then not let her do it back? What was he? Too fragile to touch? Handle with care?

Except, she didn't want to touch him, anyway. Why the hell she'd been about to do that she didn't know. He was a weirdo. A weirdo who crept up on you and disappeared into the shadows. A weirdo who was all controlling and thought everyone would jump at his command. Well, he's got another thing coming. She was here now and she was going to stay. He worked for Marie, didn't he? Not the other way round. So he couldn't make her go. Not unless Marie said so. And she wouldn't, would she?

She thumped the pillows into submission and rolled back over. He couldn't make her do anything. Oh, God, how had he turned her on like that, making her stomach curl, her nipples prickle, made her burn hotly one minute and go goose-bump cold the next? Simon didn't do that.

Damn the man, Simon did do that. Well, kind of that. When they'd made love it was nice, relaxing. He'd made her come. A nice rolling orgasm that unknotted the tension and sent her to sleep like a good bath would.

Just like a warm bath. Not like a hot-blooded, rampant shag that left her panting for more and begging for a rest.

Bugger. Where, the hell had that thought come from?

Had she ever had that? Most of her lovers had been like Simon, which she'd always thought made her the lucky one. She hadn't encountered any of the shits that a lot of girls she'd known had. The ones who only 'wanted it' when they were half cut, the ones who called tweaking a nipple foreplay. No, most of the sex she'd had was with men she could call friends. Well, the closest she got to friends. A life on the move had left her with no one really close, no girlfriends she could chat to and confide in. Marie had come close to that, though in the short time she'd known her. Being nomadic left you able to strike up acquaintances quickly – yeah 'acquaintance' was the word – it made you open because you didn't have time to be coy. You had to get on with it, then move on, and on, until one day…. you wanted to stop.

Hell, why had she thought this would be easy? Maybe it would be better in the morning, when she wasn't tired. When she wasn't thinking of James and how he seemed to turn her on one minute and scare her with that intense look the next. Yeah, it would be better. And she had no choice anyway. No car, no money to speak of and no one she could think of that would offer her a bed. And buried deep in the countryside with a man who didn't seem to welcome people seemed as safe a place as anywhere.

He was hot though, very hot.

Her hand snaked down between her thighs, rested on a pussy that was damp from something that wasn't perspiration. She groaned. Stroked gently with her fingertips. She hated him. She rolled over onto her side, her fingers still resting against the warmth, stroking absentmindedly, an automatic caress.

How the fuck was she going to sort out her life when there was a man like him lurking in the background, with his seductive voice, his lulling touch, just waiting to pounce?

13

## Chapter 2

There was a subtle shift in the air, a delicate scent that cut through the fresh hay and horse feed, and the bay mare shifted her body slightly as a shadow fell across her.

'You're up early.' James glanced briefly over towards the stable door as he finished securing the hay net.

She grinned self-consciously as though she half expected him to tell her off and a brief tang of guilt threaded its way through him.

'The sun wakes me up.' She shrugged as though he might think it was a stupid thing to say.

The sun always woke him up too. He didn't understand people who blocked out all daylight, confused the natural rhythm of their bodies and then relied on the jarring noise of an alarm. Well, he didn't understand it these days. Once he had been one of those people; one of the crowd who dodged nature in the search for something better.

'Did you sleep okay?'

Something flickered across her face that could have been guilt or embarrassment and she traced her finger along the top of the door, avoiding his gaze. 'Quite well.'

The mare gave him a nudge and he grinned. 'You want me to move out of the way of your breakfast, you bossy mare?'

'Who are you to call anyone bossy?' She'd got one dark eyebrow raised and a cheeky grin on her impish face.

Leaning against the stable wall, away from the shower of hay that the horse was creating with each greedy tug, he took a proper look at his interloper.

Last night he'd not been quite sure what had landed on his doorstep, apart from the fact that it was tired, angry and determined. Her shapely thighs had been on show when she'd been perched on the gate, along with slim bronzed arms and delicate wrists that looked like they would snap under the weight of her rucksack, but he could take or leave a good body. He'd seen and touched more naked skin in the last few years than was good for him.

But he'd not been able to ignore the heart-shaped face that was pale with something more than tiredness. And the overall image had left him wondering whether he should lock her out or take her in. And then she'd fallen into his arms like a spitting kitten and made his mind up for him.

Now, her dark hair hung straight around her face, big hazel eyes stared at him openly without rancour, eyes that last night had flashed tawny before darkening to the colour of moss. She was small, slim and yesterday's clinging blue dress had been replaced by faded worn denim shorts, heavy doc martens that he knew hid slender ankles, and a bright-green, skimpy vest that shouldn't have been allowed to be worn.

And he still didn't know what he was supposed to do with her for the five weeks before everyone else got back and the business re-opened. He didn't want company; he especially didn't want female company. He one hundred and one per cent didn't want female company that 'needed help'. What the hell had Marie been thinking when she'd sent the girl?

'You'll scare the horses wearing that.' The outline of small, perfectly round breasts drew his eye, her nipples hardening as he watched.

'Really? Will I?' Her eyes had widened, for a moment the doubt creeping back.

'Well they are part-way to colour blind, but I don't think even a horse could miss that.'

She laughed, genuine humour flooding a face of innocence and hope, which for a moment made him feel jaded. 'I could take it off.'

'You could.'

She coloured slightly, just enough to make her seem a tease, but not a temptress. 'So you've spoken to Marie?'

There was a note of challenge in her voice and he tried to stop the curve of his lips. Nothing like a direct approach, attack mode. 'I have.' He unlatched the stable door and she backed off, a nervous filly, unsure whether flight or fight was the preferred option.

'And?' It was slightly belligerent, like she was building herself up for a fight if he said the wrong thing.

'She forgot to tell me you were coming.' He gave a wry smile. Marie was a great boss, brilliant at her job and loving and giving, but she was scatter-brained. Except this time, he had a feeling she'd forgotten on purpose. She'd just been a touch evasive when he'd rung her last night. And when he'd put the phone down all he could hear was the soft strum of Kezia's guitar; a haunting, melancholy sound that pricked at the conscience he didn't want to have and made him wonder if his summer solitude was about to get well and truly gate-crashed. 'So you met at the yoga place?' Marie had told him the story, but he wanted to hear the other side of it to see if he could persuade her to change her mind. Or at least go away and come back in five weeks.

She seemed a nice enough girl, although he wouldn't say harmless. But this summer was about time on his own. He liked time on his own. There was always an air of peace and other worldliness here, even when the business was up and running, but it wasn't enough.

They'd all agreed that closing for the summer was the best tactic. Business was slack. No one needed lessons in sex in the summer, they were too busy doing it. Sun-drenched bodies on beaches, booze by the bucket-load, inhibitions thrown out along

16

with long work days and stress. When you're feeling good about your newly toned, slimmed, buffed and tanned body you don't need a helping hand to orgasm. So Marie and Dan had buggered off to Barcelona, or wherever it was they hid out, and even Saul and Roisin had hung up their boots. And he was happy to be stuck here. Alone. With a big sign on the gate saying 'No entry'.

Until someone decided to ignore it.

Someone who could talk for Britain.

Kezia was waiting for him to look at her again. He moved along to the next stable and flung open the door. He'd already fed and turned out the horse, and now he was looking forward to the physical side, building up a sweat as he mucked out. In peace. 'Yoga? Italy?'

'Yes.' It was hesitant. 'You don't like me, do you?'

'Nothing personal, I expected to be here on my own, that's all.'

'Diplomatic.' She stood in the doorway, watching as he picked up a pitchfork. 'She was in Capri a couple of months ago, at the retreat and I was working there. We got on, that's all. I didn't ask for a job you know.' She sounded defensive.

'Nothing wrong in asking.'

'But I didn't. She asked how long I was working there, and I told her that they were about to shut down for their holidays. So she said had I thought about coming back to the UK.' She paused, not filling in the gap that he knew existed. Marie had said the girl needed a base, was upset and needed friends who cared. 'She told me to come here and work the summer, then if I liked it I might be able to make it more permanent. I'm not really used to permanent.' She gnawed at her lip and he dumped a fork-load of muck in the barrow and paused.

'You get sacked a lot?'

She grinned and her whole face lifted and lightened, including the large sad eyes. 'Don't be daft. No, we-I've, always travelled, done different things in different places, you know.' She was looking down again and he wondered who the 'we' was. Not that it was any of his business. He was stuck here for the summer and he didn't need company. And definitely not the kind of company that needed a friend.

'So you don't plan on hanging around long then?'

'Maybe.' She shoved her hands in the pockets of her shorts and watched him through long eyelashes. 'Can't I help?'

'Suppose. Have you mucked out a stable before?'

She shook her head and the light caught her dark hair, glancing off the red and blue streaks. 'But it can't be difficult can it? I mean, it's only shovelling shit.'

He held his pitchfork out. 'There you go then, lady, start some shit-shovelling.' She flinched slightly at the weight and then stuck the fork deep into the bed.

'Christ almighty it's heavy. How the fuck…?'

'For a traveller you're clueless.'

'I'm not a traveller, or a gypsy.' She looked like she was trying to give him a haughty look, and not succeeding. 'I'm a free spirit.' Then she giggled as she tried to move the fork and failed.

He smiled. She was tiny, and she'd just tried to dig up half the bed. 'This stable's got a deep bed. Just take it off the top, here.' He stood behind her, put his hands over hers, skimming the muck off the top of the bed.

Her back was warm, pressed against the front of him, her tiny hands disappearing beneath his and a tremor of awareness ran through her as he swung to the side to empty the fork in the barrow. She glanced up at him then, dark hair framing the delicate features, a tinge of blush along her cheekbones and she was all trust and innocence, like she'd been when she'd first appeared this morning.

He bent his head and kissed her. Just one light kiss on those cute rosebud lips, and it drenched his senses with her smell and her need. He didn't mean to do it. He shouldn't have done it. But there was something in her, and James didn't know what the hell it was, but it had just dragged him right in where he didn't

18

want to go.

He'd not had a sweet kiss for a long time. Not since Chloe had gone. And he hadn't intended on having it again.

She eased her grip on the fork just like he knew she would, half-turned in his arms, stared at him with need, and moved her hands up to his chest.

Fuck. He let go of the pitchfork like it was molten metal and took a step back. Why the hell had he done that? He hadn't exactly banned kisses from his life when he moved out here, but he'd firmly limited them. The platonic kiss on the cheek and the passionate kiss during sex. He liked the taste of a woman just before she came, her kiss told him far more than her words ever did.

This was neither.

She was still in the same spot, swaying slightly, a quizzical expression on the face that had been clear.

'That didn't happen. I'll get another fork.'

'Sure.' Her tone was light, but more confused than hurt.

There was a fork across the yard, but he didn't pick it up. He gritted his teeth and walked to the bottom of the row of stables, took a breath and wondered why the hell he had a raging hard-on and why the hell he'd let himself touch her. More than that, kiss her.

It was that look of innocence, probably, a look he found hard to resist. She was a mixture of tease and doubt, of the unconventional and a need to fit the norm. But he wasn't here to reassure her, to teach her. He picked up the heaviest pitchfork he could see and strode back, wielding it like a weapon. A harder workout might help. This girl was not staying around, she was going before they'd got to the end of the day if he had anything to do with it.

As he reached the open stable door, his mobile buzzed in his pocket. He glanced at the display. Dan. Took a step back so that he could watch Kezia and have some level of privacy.

'What the fuck are you two playing at?'

'Hi to you too, mate. And we're having a good break, thanks for asking.'

'We don't need anyone to help out.' He leaned back against the wall and twirled the fork.

'Aw, come on Mr Grumpy. Marie said you'd probably have a hissy fit.'

'Then why did you send her?' He wasn't exactly angry; now his body was back under control it was more an annoyance. There had been a plan, which suited him fine. They went and had fun. He stayed behind to look after the place, not babysit.

'She needs something, someone.'

'I'm not a someone.'

Dan laughed. 'You're not wrong, but you do okay as a something. Here, talk to Marie.' He was handed over to the pacifier. Not that any of them was exactly fiery; they all knew how to defuse a situation, how not to rise to the bait. But they knew this was his weak spot; they knew that being stuck here with a woman depending on him was supposed to be out of the equation.

'You're not playing fair.' He got a word in before she did.

'Sorry.' She sighed. 'She's had a tough time, but she's nice. The clients will like her, they loved her in Capri. She's got a gentle touch, she's natural, no artifice, open.'

'You don't need to spell it out, I can read—'

'I know, you're better than me at understanding people, but I'm just trying to explain. I couldn't leave her, James.' Her voice was soft. 'Help me to help her, please? Look after her, once she was out of that job she needed something straight away, trust me.' Oh, great, someone desperate, one of Marie's fallen angels who needed rescuing, putting back together again. Except she didn't look like she was falling apart. She had guts, was prepared to fight her battles and stand her ground. Even if she was tiny and had great big eyes that shone out with a naivety and purity you didn't often see these days. Especially not here.

'So, why didn't you tell me? And why didn't you come back to sort it yourself?'

She laughed. 'She needs someone like you, and she needs time

20

to understand the place before we get clients back in. And,' she paused, laughed, 'I forgot.'

'You haven't given her a job description, have you?'

'She'll be fine. We'll find her something to do.'

'Marie.' It was his turn to sigh. So he was trapped here for the summer with a girl, except nobody had told her what the job was. Once she knew what went on she'd probably go, like Roisin nearly had. But go where? Either way he'd look the bastard. Whether he cornered her into staying or chased her away. 'And how do you know she'll be any use?'

'We'll find something for her to do. She's sweet, she'll put people at ease.' Another pause. 'She's got nowhere to go James, no money, nothing.'

And no one from the sound of it.

The sigh travelled across the miles. 'Do you want me to come back?'

Great, that would mean two of them here to bother him. 'I know you don't mean that Marie, so I'm not even going to say no. You've got a soft spot for her for her haven't you?'

'You might get one too if you give her a chance.'

'You know I haven't got any spot to appeal to, so why are you trying? I don't do waifs and strays.'

'She's neither. She's sad, broke and needs a job. Go on, be nice to her.'

She had an air of melancholy to her that was for sure, from the way she'd played her guitar last night, like it really meant something to her. But sad? 'I'm not a babysitting service.' And she's not a baby, far, far from a baby.

'Will you at least be nice and find her something to do? Pretty please?' He heard the chink of glasses in the background. 'See what she thinks? And even if she's not interested in staying long term, she can help out with the horses until we get back, which will give her a bit of cash.'

'I was quite happy sorting the horses on my own, thanks.'

'Roisin might even take her on as a stable hand. I bet she's good with animals.'

He laughed. 'You should see her with a pitchfork. I'll catch you later.' He flicked the phone off before she got a chance to say anything else, and took the handful of strides to the other side of the yard. And the girl, no, woman, who he seemed to be lumbered with.

'Were you hoping I'd finish it before you got back?' Her voice was soft, a question that went beyond the stable duties.

'At the rate you work? No chance.' He smiled, hoping it looked at least halfway to good-natured, swung the fork off his shoulder and stripped his shirt over his head.

She wolf-whistled.

'You watch what you're getting into, girl.' He waved an admonishing finger at her and she gave him the Vs. 'You watch it yourself, Mister.'

Hmm, any minute now and he'd be tempted to put her over his knee if she carried on the teasing. 'Let's move on to the next box. You're getting better.'

'Couldn't get much worse you mean?'

'Something like that.' He watched as she got into the swing of it, lifting her fork more easily and with a steady rhythm now she knew what she was doing and every now and then she'd catch him looking and stick her tongue out or just grin.

For a lost and lonely girl she had a self-confidence that surprised him, and she worked hard, not pausing to chat or flirt like the other girls did.

'So, what do you do here?' They'd emptied the wheelbarrow for the last time and were putting the beds back down. 'It isn't just horses, is it?'

'What did Marie tell you?'

She tucked a long strand of hair behind her ear and pursed her lips. 'Well.' She put her head on one side as though waiting for inspiration.

'I'll take that as not a lot then. So you came all this way for a job you know jack all about?'

'I trusted Marie.' She looked straight at him. 'Are you saying I shouldn't have?'

'No, not exactly. Do you trust everyone you meet, then?'

'Unless they give me a reason not to, Mr Cynical. And, anyhow, I hadn't got anything else lined up, I've got to do something, so why not this?' Her small shoulders went up in a shrug.

'But what's "this?" Stable hand?'

'Well, what do you do?'

'I'm a sex therapist.'

She laughed, carried on tossing straw in the air. 'You're a sex therapist?'

'Yup, that's what I do here, what we all do.'

The straw lost her attention. 'You are kidding, right?' Her eyes narrowed. 'You're not. Wow.' She leaned on the fork and eyed him up like she hadn't seen him before. 'But you're a man.'

'Well-spotted. Does that mean I don't qualify to know about sex?'

'Well, no, but… So, if you're a sex therapist what does that make me?'

'Good question. Chief shit shoveller?

'I can do other things as well, you know.' The glare she gave him was steelier than he expected. 'So, you get wackos here who are sexaholics? Or can't get it up and stuff?'

'We get normal people like you and me who want better sex lives.'

She looked directly at him, her eyes slightly wider and gave a short, incredulous snort. 'You don't need to teach people about sex, you just do it, right? Sex is just sex.'

'Not necessarily.' He tucked his hands into his pockets and leaned back against the wall. 'People don't always know what good sex is, or how to ask someone to please them.'

She'd coloured up a bit, but wasn't backing down. 'Bollocks. I mean I wouldn't go to a sex therapist. I mean if you like someone enough to sleep with them, then it's just going to happen isn't it.'

'Is it? Is sex always the same for you, whoever you do it with?'

Her colour shifted another notch up the scale towards red hot. 'Yes, well no. Well, it just works better sometimes than other times.' She shrugged. 'Depends how much you fancy someone I suppose.'

'Have you never been left high and dry, wanting more?'

'I'm fine with a cuddle, I don't have to, you know…'

'Come?' God, how he would just love to take her here and now, to show her what passion was really about. He pushed off from the wall and took a step towards her, and she flinched, but didn't move away.

'I could make you come.'

'I can make myself come thanks, no big deal there.'

'I can make you come,' He took another step closer. Stroked along her lip with one finger, 'without touching you where you want me to most.'

'Slightly bigger deal, but if I get in the zone, think the right things…..' Her voice tailed off as eased his thumb between her teeth.

He shouldn't, he should keep his distance. But she was turning him on something rotten. She was all feisty and sassy, but there was also a streak of the submissive about her. A streak he didn't want to ignore. He'd forgotten what 'pure' meant after he'd walked out on his home, his job, his wife. And every woman since had been just there for the sex. And every woman in the future would be. And he wasn't going to start anything with Kezia, he just wanted to show her. No, he just wanted her. To see her surrender, for him. To him.

'All you have to do, is say please.' James paused. There was hesitation in her eyes, but she'd stilled, gone quiet. Was waiting. And it was making his balls tingle in a way he'd almost forgotten existed.

He traced along the top edge of her teeth with his salty thumb and Kezia wanted to say please. Well, more like shout it out. Not to any arty-farty sex therapist crap, but to a good, hard shag. His hard-on was straining against his jeans and she could smell him; pure sex. Yes, he scared her, he was so friggin' intense, but he turned her on as well. Like she'd been turned on when she was a teenager and thought her Mum was just about to walk in on her and a guy and find out they weren't just listening to music. Like she was turned on when she imagined being pinned down, helpless, as the man she'd always loved forced her to submit to his every desire. Or something like that. Shit, books and films had a lot to answer for. She touched his finger with the tip of her tongue. He was staring straight into her eyes, his own so dark she couldn't tell where his pupils ended and the colour began.

'Do you want me?' He eased his thumb from her mouth, squeezed her lower lip between thumb and finger, gently tugging and by the way it was affecting her swollen breasts he could well have been tugging her nipples. He let his hand drift down to rest lightly on her chin.

'I don't know you.' Her throat had tightened with anticipation for what would come next, her shoulders tense.

'But you want me, in the same way I want you.'

He slid his hand under her hair, ran one finger from the base of her neck up to where it met her skull, pressing gently into the soft indent and she couldn't stop the shudder that travelled down her spine pooling at the base. That was good. His thumb circled, small persistent needy circles that sent a pulse between her legs. She gasped. Now could be the time to say please, or thank you. Oh that was very good, he seemed to have found the spot that channelled right down to orgasm central and if he stopped now she might have to scream.

'Have you ever had sex with a stranger?' And that husky voice was the icing on the cake, or should that be the cherry?

He'd said something. What was it? Oh, yeah. Sex, stranger. 'I make love, not have sex.' She could barely hear her own whisper, she swayed slightly into the pressure of his hand. 'And nobody I'd call strange.' Slightly wacky, yes, but not strange. She wanted to reach out and hold him, but she just knew it would break the spell. He'd stop. She didn't want him to stop.

'Just having sex can be good.'

She shivered under his touch as his thumb ran along the side of her neck, resting over her pulse point. His large, warm hand cradled her head, her jaw in the palm of his hand. If this was sex then fine, bring it on.

'But it's not—'

'You've made love to people you're not in love with.'

It didn't seem to be a question, and right now her vocal chords didn't want to play anyway.

'That's comfort, not a real connection, and what happens when you can't be bothered to be a comfort blanket any longer?' His fingers were still doing their thing and her brain seemed to be slowly melting, which gave him an unfair advantage.

'But I—'

'Close your eyes.' It must have been surprise, no way would she have just shut them otherwise. His fingers slowly moved down to her throat, with the lightest of touch. 'Clasp your hands behind your back.' Hell, she did that too. But if she didn't she couldn't find out what came next, and all of a sudden she wanted to know.

His breath was warm against her skin, he must be close, so close. She had to touch him, she mustn't touch him. The nip of his teeth on her neck made her jump, then whimper. His finger was tracing down her chest, down towards her breasts and her nipples started to prickle. She just had to reach out, hold him, or something.

'Don't move.' Shit, all she'd done was think about it, unclasped her hands just a touch, but that liquid chocolate voice in her ear made her freeze and her stomach tighten.

His finger traced a path around her breast, slowly, tantalisingly moving in with each circle, then outwards, never touching the hard nub. She needed him to touch her nipples, or suck them, or anything... Any second now she really was going to scream. He moved on to the other breast and she could hear her breath coming in short gasps, feel her heart pounding so heavily her whole body seemed to be shaking with it. She bit her lip. She wasn't going to beg.

His warm hands moved down, circling her waist, firm fingers pressing down over her stomach, lower, lower. He was holding her hips now, and those probing thumbs were circling her stomach just above her mound. Firm, tantalising. She moaned as she felt her juices pool in her knickers whimpering as she clenched her thighs together, feeling the slow pulsing in her pussy build. Oh, God she was going to come. She couldn't stop now, she couldn't. Her knees were trembling, she tightened her stomach muscles, felt the delicious throb intensify.

And he stopped. Let go. Cold air replaced where his hands had been.

'Wha–?' For a split second she was dazed, still numbed by the soft, sensual throbbing that had been bubbling its way through her body. She stared at him, confused, and he stared straight back, from a safe distance.

'Demonstration over.'

'Demonstration?' The calm words hit her hard, her muscles contracting for a far different reason from a few minutes ago. The bastard. He'd shoved his hands back in his pockets, partly to hide his hard-on, and his face was devoid of expression. So, he hadn't been pulled to her like she had to him, this wasn't about the way her body reacted when he came within ten yards of her. This was business, pure and simple, showing her what a fucking clever sex quack he was. And she'd just started thinking he was nice. So much for her being a good judge of character.

'Yup. That's what we do here, Kezia.'

She shook her head slowly, fighting the burn of tears that was building up in her eyes. Sexual frustration and emotions warred

27

in her body. 'You sad bastard.' She took a step backwards, back against the wall, her sweating palms against the cold plaster. He'd got under her skin, made her give up control, just to prove his point that love and lust were a million miles apart.

He didn't move as she stared at him, didn't flinch, but the empty look in his eyes made her want to grab him, shake him, scream at him until he snapped out of it. It had felt real, he'd felt real, warm, like he wanted to create something between them.

An illusion and a control freak.

One tear spilled and she could feel the damp heat trickle down her cheek, taste the salt in her mouth. Not bothering to wipe the tear or say a word she finally found the power to move her feet, push past him.

'Kezia.' But she didn't pause, didn't turn, she just kept on at the same steady pace across the yard, forcing herself not to run, until she couldn't hear him or the horses any more.

Kezia kicked off her boots in the kitchen, hardly pausing, then marched straight up the stairs, banging the door shut and falling on to the bed.

What the hell was wrong with her? Why had she let him get under her skin? Some stupid fantasy about domineering men and wild passionate sex that a stupid corner of her mind had decided was about to come true. Except she didn't want a domineering man. And definitely not one who wouldn't even let her touch him.

She stared up at the ceiling. He'd barely touched her breasts and he definitely hadn't touched the place she wanted him to most. He hadn't kissed her, he hadn't talked dirty to her and he hadn't fucked her. He'd just breathed in her ear and stroked her. And she'd just had what she was pretty sure could have turned into one hell of an orgasm, if he hadn't stopped it before it had barely begun. That feeling in her belly, the gentle pulsing between her thighs had been slowly unravelling something deep inside, and she'd wanted the tremble spreading through her body to go on forever.

28

And now, she was just left with a dull ache that needed satisfying.

She shouldn't have let him touch her. He was an attention-seeking, arrogant, domineering twat with a chip on his shoulder the size of a small skyscraper. Getting off on being able to turn women on. And, oh my God, right now she wanted more of the idiot.

Leaning over she grabbed her rucksack and pulled a battered notepad out of the back, ignoring her mobile, which was beeping with yet another incoming text. There was only one person who it could be from; Simon. Simon, who had agreed she needed space, who had agreed that they didn't have a future together as lovers, but should stay in touch as friends. Simon, who was starting to become a pain in the arse. Yeah, his 'hope you got there okay' texts were fine, but then the follow-ups, along the lines of 'I need you, when are you heading back?' and 'you need me, I know you do' had sounded desperate and had unnerved her. And they were starting to get irritating. He hadn't been like that when they were together, he'd been laid back and casual, they'd taken things one day at a time. No expectations, no demands, no needs. What was going to come next? 'I can't live without you?'

Simon had been fun, the brother she'd never had, more friend than lover. They'd had a few weeks of laughs, cuddles and getting to know you shags, but never once had there been the slightest hint that he was expecting more out of the relationship than she was. Saying goodbye had been hard, because she did care, but in her heart she'd always known that they were happy for now, not forever. And she'd thought he'd felt the same.

Until she'd shown him the plane ticket. Then he'd flipped a bit, which had shocked her, almost cried, which had shocked her even more and now was bugging her. Staying friends would have been great, but this wasn't. He seemed to have turned overnight from casual dude without a care in the world to someone bordering on obsessive. Stalker material.

She pushed the phone further into the rucksack and fished out a pen. She was crap at spelling, and even worse at long words, but she'd started scribbling down what she was up to after they had gone. Her parents. At first she'd just told them, spoken out loud each night when she was lying in bed, telling them what she'd done, thought, hoped. And then it seemed easier to write it down, when she was sharing digs with people who already thought she was bonkers. And muttering to herself labelled her as completely deranged.

This time it wasn't for them, though, this was for her. It looked like she was stuck with this guy for the summer, just the two of them. Which could have been cool, but it looked like it was heading for hell, probably because of the sizzle every time she went near him. But she wasn't in the habit of hating people. She took them as she found them and accepted people's differences. It was what she'd been brought up to do, *he can be an earl or a tramp darling*, her mother had always drummed into her, *but it's what's inside that counts. We're all human, even if we're trying our damnedest not to be. And if we are, then there's a reason, and we're not always going to know it or understand it. But we can accept it.*

Yeah. Easy for her to say. Kezia liked to know, though, not just accept. And right now she wanted to know how the heck she was going to survive the summer with Mr Moody, without either wanting to kill him or jump him.

The last bit could be tricky, but he didn't want jumping. Obviously. The last thing on his mind was a fun fling that involved cuddles and kisses. The man just wanted sex, and preferably without his cock being involved in the party. Wacky.

So, she needed a plan. Step one; write down all the positives, ignore the negatives because she'd end up with a whole book full of them and as she couldn't run away yet. There wasn't any point going there.

*Positives* (she underlined it for good measure) – *nice place, in the middle of nowhere, Marie back soon (oh, God five more weeks of him), comfy bed, sweet horses, money (essential), food (essential), he's sexy (very), he's hot.*

*Plan – admire the scenery (him included, note to self – handy for fantasies), learn how to ride, muck out the stables (and anything else he says), try to ignore the way he looks at me, DON'T let him touch me (she underlined the DON'T as well for extra good measure), find a job with horses.*

*Another note to self (v. important) – make sure never to go near a sex therapist again (Marie is OK).*

Her list covered the finding a job part of her goal, the making something out of her life part, but not the settling down. It didn't look like this was the place for that, but it was a start.

She let her arm fall back onto the bed and felt calmer. She had a plan.

And now she really must finish off what he'd started, or she was going to feel frustrated, randy and rampant when she saw him again. The last thing she wanted to feel was sex-starved, especially if she was going to stick to the plan.

Closing her eyes she pulled down the zipper on her jeans, and *kerpow,* he was there in her head like the magic genie. Standing up against her in the stable. She eased her hand into her panties, let her fingers rest against the damp, swollen lips.

*'Turn around.' She turned to face the wall without question. 'Take your top off.' For a second she hesitated. 'Now.'*

*'Yes, sir.' She peeled the damp top over her head, let it dangle from one hand, unsure what to do. 'Move your legs apart.' Slowly she edged her heavy boots apart until they were hip-width, wide enough for him to touch her if he chose to.*

Kezia let the tip of her finger ease its way inside herself.

*'Hold your hands behind your back.' Before she could object he'd bound her wrists with her t-shirt. He moved closer until she could feel the heat of his body only centimetres away. All he needed to do was sway his body and he would cover the gap between them so that skin met skin. But he didn't. 'Don't worry, trust me, I won't do anything you don't want me to.' Oh, but she wanted, wanted so much.*

*He swept her hair up in one hand, twisted it so that her neck*

31

was exposed and then he kissed her. He smelled of soap, of herbal shampoo, clean and inviting, and of salt, of need and lust. Slowly he ran his tongue down her spine, her shoulder blades tightened and a shiver ran all the way from top to bottom. 'You can say stop, but I want to show you what you've never let yourself have, what you've never let someone give you.'

'I want—'

'Shh. Don't move and don't speak unless you want me to stop.' He let her hair fall, tucked it over her shoulder so that it left her back uncovered, exposed. She heard him strip his top off, and she wanted to look at him, but the second she tilted her head he took hold of her hair. 'I said don't move, unless you want me to stop. Do you want me to stop?'

'No, no don't stop.' His firm thumbs stroked down either side of her spine, a slow, steady pressure that made her gasp and her buttocks clench, he was already finding the spots that made her want him, need him. This time he circled his thumb as he went, his splayed fingers curling around her rib cage. As he got lower, ever lower towards the base of her spine she tightened her thighs.

'Don't.' He stopped, waiting until she'd relaxed. 'Accept it, let your body ask for it.' He bent down, slowly licked her linked fingers, then took each thumb in turn into his mouth, teasing with his teeth, sucking, taking each finger in turn and letting her rock her hips. She shifted back towards him.

She stroked her fingers inside a pussy that was already tensing.

'Naughty girl. Rest your forehead on the wall and shift your feet back a bit.' Her weight was forward now, her thighs tight and trembling as he ran first his finger, and then his tongue, up each toned inner thigh. And then he tasted her thighs properly, circled the softness of her skin, just inside her shorts, with his tongue, kissing, sucking, nibbling as his thumbs traced ever firmer circles over her buttocks, the very base of her spine and she knew that she was going to come. She could smell her own scent, feel the tremble that was under his hands, spreading upwards, mingling with the anticipation and want.

'*Let go.*' He rested his hand between her legs, felt the heat and dampness through her shorts, pressed against her, let her rock against him.

'*Oh, shit.*' Her thighs tightened around his hand and she was coming.

Kezia gasped as her body hit the high it had been aiming for. Her pussy tightened greedily around her fingers. Gradually the tremors died down, her body fizzled back down from its peak, leaving just a gentle buzz of warmth. Then she rolled over on to her side and crashed.

# Chapter 3

'You're going?'

'No, what gave you that idea?' She filled the kettle and put it down with a heavy clatter, hoping that it hid the sound of her heart hammering away sixty to the dozen. Feeling light-headed could be put down to the orgasm he'd inadvertently given her last night. Feeling hot and bothered was definitely down to him just being there. He was dressed in jeans that hugged his hips like they were never going to let go, and an open-necked shirt with rolled-up sleeves that declared 'man alert.'

'I just thought…'

'Ah, it can be a dangerous thing, thinking.'

She could have sworn he was on the verge of laughing at her, but then his still eyes darkened. 'What upset you yesterday?'

Oh, so that's why he thought she was going. *You mean apart from feeling used and abused? Nah, she'd let that one go.* 'I was thinking about my parents.' Fuck him if he thought the whole sex thing was about him, he might have a certain amount of control over her body, but if he thought he could control her mind then he could think again.

'While that was happening?'

'While that was happening.' She dumped a spoonful of coffee in a mug. 'I miss them, that's all.' Day to day she could cope, but when her defences were down, when someone hit a nerve and opened her up, it still hurt. He'd made her feel vulnerable, he'd reminded her that she had no one to run to. She was all on her own. Sink or swim. 'Okay, explain this whole mind, body, soul shit that you were going on about. But skip the practical demonstrations this time.'

'What mind, body and soul shit?' He was smiling a lazy smile that was reminding a spot between her thighs, high up between her thighs, about yesterday.

'When I was asking about your sex therapy malarkey, you said it probably wasn't a million miles from the whole yoga retreat thing, the mind etcetera, etcetera stuff.'

'Did I?'

'You did.'

'Do you remember everything anyone says?' He pushed his chair back from the table, stretched out his never-ending legs. Well they were actually ending, one end in brown boots, and the other end at a distinctly swollen crotch, which she tried not to stare at. Was the man permanently in a state of ready-alert? Is that what being so into sex did to you? She glanced back up at the amused face.

'If it might come in handy.'

'You really want to know?'

'I do.'

'Thinking of coming into the business now?'

'No way.' She dropped her voice, with an effort, back to normal decibels. 'I mean, no. I was just interested, that's all.'

'You know much about yoga or Buddhism then?'

'Nope. I know nothing about anything.' She could feel that stupid feeling rise up, except he didn't look like he thought she was stupid. 'Old thicko me.'

'You don't strike me as thick – you seem quite smart really.' He was looking at her so intently now she felt like she was just about to be tried and sentenced, or at the very least interrogated. 'Why do you say that?'

'We never stayed anywhere long enough to go to school, so when I did make an appearance, everyone took the piss. Mum ended up saying she'd teach me herself.'

'So?'

'I don't really read papers, I can't tell you what GDP is, I never read any proper books, I've not got any qualifications really, or anything.' She shrugged and avoided looking at him. 'I want to get a proper job, stay in one place and learn stuff.' *Feel safe.*

'You can learn a lot of stuff not staying in one place.' He was sounding almost civilised, and like he vaguely meant it.

She glanced up, but he didn't seem to be judging her. 'I bet you went to a good school didn't you? You know what to say at dinner parties, read the papers, know which knife to butter the bread with, so how can you know how I feel?'

'Dinner parties are vastly over-rated, so are butter knives.'

'So, the mind and body stuff?' she said, attempting to change the direction this conversation was taking. She didn't really want to talk about her dreams with anyone else, sharing them spoiled them. They'd never happen if she spelled them out, if she had to explain them.

'I used to work in an office, Kezia. It isn't all good you know, the learning, the politics. In fact it's crap. It's a rat race and I didn't want to be a rat. Be yourself, not who you think other people want you to be.'

'Fine.' He'd never understand. She didn't know who the hell she was supposed to be. He'd got roots, got a home and he knew stuff. And she didn't know anything. It was easy to throw away these sort of things once you had them, but it was harder if they'd never been there in the first place. 'So, this isn't your place then?'

'No, I'm just the paid help.'

'Do Marie and Dan own it?' Which meant it was up to them whether she got a job or not.

'Nope.'

'Nope?'

'Nosy aren't you?'

'Well, this might shock you a bit, but I have been called persistent. Mum used to say if you want to know something send Kez.' Her mother hadn't really been that bothered about finding out what people thought or did, she used to laugh at the way Kezia pestered until she got an answer. Her mother just trusted that if she needed to know something the facts would come out sooner or later. But the facts hadn't come out soon enough when it really mattered, or she'd still be here, wouldn't she? Kezia felt that familiar lump start to form in her throat, she swallowed it down, tried to ignore the knowing look that had crept into his eyes. 'So, who does own it?' The lump softened, moved down to the place in her heart where it normally rested.

'A couple called Roisin and Saul. She runs the stables.'

'Oh.' So maybe it was Roisin she needed to impress. 'Why did you ditch the office?' She rested her chin on her hands and ignored the mildly exasperated look on his face, but he seemed to have decided to humour her.

'I wanted something more in life.' For a moment she could swear there was a slightly bleak look in his face, but it cleared too fast to remember it, pin it down. 'I worked in IT, went to the office every day.' He wasn't looking at her now, he was focused on a spot beyond her. Way beyond. 'Got married, did the dinner parties and the conferences. It was all a pile of mundane shit.' His gaze shifted back to the present, and her.

'Okay.' Probably best not to question the marriage bit, or any other part of the 'mundane shit' right now. 'So you came here?' He half nodded. 'And what do you do now that's so good? Amaze me.' He was staring, unmoving, but he looked like he might be unbending. She tried a smile. 'Please.'

He grinned, his smile a mix of mischief and tease that was at odds with the quiet way he'd been looking at her before. 'Oh, so you can say "please" after all.'

'I can.' She smiled back, how could she stop herself? 'I can even beg if I think it might be worth it.'

He laughed. He was nice when he lost that brooding edge, she thought. She stopped feeling like she was some kind of exotic dinner laid out for him to nibble at, at will. Okay, scrap the nibble word – that was *so* not a good thought when he was around.

'Go on, tell me all about the mind, body and soul crap.'

'So which bit of the mind, body and soul crap, as you so nicely put it, did you want to talk about?'

'Just the bits you think I'll get. I'm intrigued.'

'I'm intrigued too.' He lifted an eyebrow slightly and gave her the sort of roguish look she didn't want to see.

'Go on, Mr Sexpert, open my mind.'

'That isn't necessarily my main interest.' The chuckle caught her unawares. He was good at that, too good, creeping up under her defences. 'It's the surrendering that interests me.' His eyes narrowed slightly.

She wasn't going to blush. Whatever he said, she was going to be cool. Think cucumber. No, think ice. Ice worked. Cucumber didn't.

'I'd love to know what's going on in that head.'

'None of your business. Anyhow, it might scare you.' Not that she could imagine him being scared of anything. 'Can we get back to the sex?' Why did her mouth love to go out on a limb and work independently? 'As in mind stuff, of course, and not the 'what's going on in my head' bit.'

'Of course. Okay, apart from at the moment, I think you're pretty open aren't you?' It was obviously rhetorical. 'But most people these days aren't; they spend half their lives pretending to be someone else. Wife, husband, parent, boss, the best worker in the world, it's all about artifice and front. But good sex is about being open and sometimes people need to relearn that bit.'

'But—'

'I'm getting on to that bit in a minute.' He grinned. God, he was sexy. Dark, still, almost animal like. Animal magic. Who needed shape-shifters? 'People need to surrender.' He winked.

'I bet you haven't.'

'What makes you say that?' A hint of broodiness had crept back in. Damn, he was so bloody sensitive, it was like playing with a box of duff fireworks, a fizzle one minute, then deadly sparks the next.

'You won't let anyone near enough to get to know the real you.'

'What you see is what you get.'

'But it isn't the real you.'

His face had hardened a bit. Maybe she was pushing her luck and he was about to clam up on her and come over all scary again. Saying what she thought had got her into trouble more than once. People didn't like you being open, but it was him that had started it.

'I'm open, it is the real me.'

'The Great Untouchable?' It bugged her the way he'd flinched when she'd reached out to him. Really bugged her. Bugged her the way he was going on about being open, but was as tight as a clam.

There was a wry lift to the corner of his mouth. He crossed his arms, which just about summed it up. 'See. I don't know much, but I know that if you cross your arms you're hiding stuff.'

He shook his head slightly with what could have been exasperation but kept his arms folded. 'Your mind is how you think, your knowledge, understanding, your past and emotions, but not really your heart. Without opening your mind, surrendering your thoughts, and allowing someone to know you, you can't connect.'

Okay, so surrendering her mind *might* be up for grabs. 'But, not your heart? Open mind, closed heart?'

He ignored that. 'Your body is the physical part, of course.' He was staring at her in that unerring way, the panther about to strike or walk disdainfully away. 'Surrendering your body is not about agreeing to share it, it's about giving up control, letting someone touch you wherever they want, trusting them. Letting go frightens people; they don't know how to do it. Sometimes it's easier to let a stranger in than a friend. Or a lover.'

'But anything could happen, you can't just let someone do

whatever they want to you, especially someone you don't know.' He'd touched her and she'd let go, but it had been a mistake. Massive mistake. Tick that one off the list.

'You're not vulnerable if you trust someone. And your soul is what makes you who you are, the power deep inside, your passion, emotions—'

'You said that was mind.'

He ignored her. 'It's your spirit, the bit that you have to dig deep inside to find, some people believe it never changes, but others say that there is nothing permanent about it and that we should let our soul be altered, let it grow.' His voice had gradually become more distanced, as though he was reciting some mantra and he didn't know if he believed in it any more. 'Surrender your soul and you risk everything.'

'You're spooking me out a bit now.'

His dark gaze refocused on her. 'I don't think I am.' His voice was soft, so soft, like a caress that you didn't know was there until it had gone. 'We can all surrender if we find the right person, trust someone enough.' His eyes narrowed slightly and there was the slightest flinch in his voice, which made her wonder whether he'd ever found that person. But something warned her not to ask.

And he *was* spooking her. His words had this edge to them that was hard to resist. An edge that said her fantasies could be closer to reality than she wanted them to be. 'And you want me to surrender all of that to you?'

'I don't want you to do anything.'

'Then, what?'

'You asked.' He grinned at her, one hundred per cent back in the present, and swallowed a large mouthful of coffee. 'That's why,' he cocked an eyebrow, 'sex isn't just sex.'

'Smart arse.'

He laughed easily.

'So you aren't going to be throwing your weight about if I stay and do this job?'

'You seemed to like it when I threw my weight around yesterday.'

'So? It doesn't mean I want to be bossed around by a man.' *By you, actually.*

'Are you sure?' He leaned forward, his forearms on the table and she wasn't quite sure if he was winding her up or flirting. But he wasn't the type of man who did flirting.

'Which bit of *I don't want to be bossed around* didn't you understand?'

'Do you ever do as you're told?'

'Not often. Well, not if I feel like I've been taken advantage of.'

'And did you?'

'I don't know.' And she didn't. She didn't know if she'd enjoyed it, wanted it, been liberated by it. Or if she felt manipulated. Sure, he understood her body, but did that mean he should do that? Did she want him to? She was damned if she knew. Which was pathetic.

Sex for her had always been part of affection, not always love, but something close. It was a shared experience, a give and take. Yeah, she admitted that she wasn't going to say no to someone she fancied just because they weren't destined to be her happy-ever-after. But she wanted a closeness, a shared part of a relationship – even if the relationship was transient. And he thought sex was a tool. He'd tapped into her in a way she didn't want to be messed with. If they'd just had a shag it would have been fine. Well, not fine, but better. Maybe.

'I'm sorry about yesterday.' That surprised her. Him apologising. 'I was out of line.'

'I don't want to lay myself bare to someone I hardly know.' And that was her way of apologising. *You made me feel an idiot.* She wasn't going to say it, though. 'Now you've proved your point, maybe I should stick with the mucking-out duties.' *As long as I don't get an insatiable urge to be bossed around again.*

At least she'd slept last night, like a log, after ramping up her fantasies into unknown territory. Which was a bonus. Every cloud, as they say.

41

'Do sex therapists ever just get on with it and shag like normal people as well?'

He laughed, a full, hearty laugh that made something secretive in her stomach curl up in delight. She smiled back, she couldn't help it. 'Not the clients. By the way, can you ride a horse? Ever done it?'

Hmm, the opening up, talking bit was obviously over. 'Well yes, years ago when I was on holiday. But I mean, it's only sitting there isn't it? It can't be that hard.'

'Here we go again. Nothing is ever that hard is it?'

'Am I being stupid?'

'The only stupid bit about you is maybe believing that.' He stood, walked on silent feet to the sink and put his empty mug down. 'Enough philosophy for one day, drink up and we'll go and exercise the horses.'

'Exercise?'

'I'll lunge you on Sparky and see if it's safe to let you loose on him.'

Sparky was big. Something called Sparky should be small and cute, a Thelwell scaled up a bit, like the ponies they gave you to hack out on when you were on holiday. Everything about him was big, nothing about him was cute.

'How the fuck am I supposed to get on that?'

James had tacked the horse up while she'd stood as far away as she could, hoping the distance would shrink him. It didn't.

'Don't worry, you'll be fine.' His voice was mild, still at the level he used when he talked to the horses.

'I'm not worried.'

'Good, but don't. Relax, or he'll know.'

Shit, what did 'he'll know' mean?

'You don't have to do this if you don't want.'

'I said I'm not worried. But I still don't see how the hell—'

'I'll give you a leg up. I just want you to relax and do exactly what I say and you'll be fine. Trust me.'

He straightened up from messing around with buckles and stirrups and his dark eyes met her full on. It was half challenge, all authority. He was looking at as though like he could solve everything, take care of her. She finally realised what 'in control' meant. And the smallest hint of what trust could be filtered into her mind.

She took the step forward, raised her leg so that the warmth of his hand could wrap around her calf, felt his strength as he seemed to effortlessly lift her onto the horses' back.

'Good. Now close your eyes.'

Hell, if this was what surrender was about she had a horrible feeling she wasn't going to like it one bit.

'Trust me.'

She closed her eyes, clutching the pommel of the saddle as the horse lurched forward.

'And breathe. Breathing is important.' She heard the smile in his voice. 'Talk to me.'

'Since when did "talk to me" start a decent conversation?'

He laughed. 'Count each step until you get in the rhythm. I thought you said you'd ridden before?'

'A while ago.' She unpeeled her fingers a bit from the hard leather. Quite a while ago, but who was counting the years? 'And it wasn't with my eyes shut.'

James let the lunge rope out a little longer and watched as colour trickled back into her knuckles and the tension leached away bit by bit from her body. She was a natural, and she was gorgeous. She was like a small beacon of positivity that kept nudging at him, begging him to open his eyes and mind to possibilities that he tried so hard to keep locked away.

Her body rocked in perfect time with the footfall of the horse, absorbing the energy, completely in tune. And that was what kept drawing him back into her circle. There wasn't a trace of artifice, no layers to break down.

He'd been a bastard, which didn't shock him. But it hurt, and that bit most definitely did surprise him. He'd taken advantage, overstepped the mark just to try and drive home to her that sex and affection were miles apart. That with him it was all about the first, and he didn't need the second.

After she'd stormed off he'd been left with an emptiness and a strange feeling of regret. Her green-brown eyes had been flooded with tears and a pain that he didn't understand, a pain he could see ran deep inside her. If he'd done that to someone like Chloe it would have been nearly okay, but doing it to her was wrong. Chloe was all about games. And now he'd lowered himself to her level.

He'd wanted to keep Kezia at a distance, wanted to chase her away so he could go back to his cave. And she'd just bounced back with a smile. Every time. Sweet, open and determined to do what she'd come for. Even if it meant clambering over an obstacle like him.

'Can I open my eyes yet?'

'Nope. You up to going a bit faster?'

'Go for it, Mr Bossy Boots.' She was grinning. He shifted his body slightly, it was all he needed to do to tell old Sparky to shift into canter, and the horse responded instantly, striking off into an effortless, even lope that he knew wouldn't feel fast. 'Yay.' She opened her eyes, twisting her body slightly to look at him and caught the horse with her heel. Sparky was safe as houses, but he felt the nudge, gave a small buck of surprise and she fell – like a relaxed sack of spuds onto the sand covered floor. She rolled towards him, laughing.

The horse pulled up automatically, glanced at James as though to say 'wasn't my fault, mate,' then dropped his head.

'I told you not to open your eyes.' He tried to look stern, but had a distinct feeling he'd failed.

She was lying on her back, giggling up at him, rocking her knees from side to side and he couldn't help but grin back. He knelt down. 'Nothing hurt?' Running one hand slowly up her booted calf, he stopped at her knee.

'You want to give me a full examination?'

He stared down at her face, watched it slowly sober up. He would love to give her a full examination. There was the slightest play of a smile on her lips, the slightest hint of doubt in her eyes.

'Kiss me.'

He shouldn't. He needed her to understand that his time for fun-filled summers of love and sex ended years ago. That getting involved wasn't for him.

'Stop thinking. Don't say anything.' She tilted her head slightly to one side so that his gaze was drawn to the long, slender neck that had tasted so good. 'Just kiss me, please.'

So he did.

# Chapter 4

His touch was unexpected, even though she'd been lying there like a hussy begging him to do it. She really didn't expect him to, even though he was looking at her like he might, even though his hand had tightened on her knee.

Saying it was just inviting him to say no. But she could take that, because she wasn't supposed to let him near her anyway. It was on the plan, do NOT let him touch. With a capital NOT. But hey, plans were made to be changed.

And she wanted him. Boy, did she want him.

He moved closer, slipped one hand under her head and her scalp tingled.

Then his head dropped, dry, insistent lips met hers and everything else tingled. His mouth was firm and instantly demanding, not the hesitant sloppy need she'd had before and as she parted her lips automatically, his taste filtered into her senses. A mingle of coffee, mint and of hay and lust hit her and she didn't know whether it was smell or taste. It surrounded her, entered her, made her forget where she was and why. And it flicked the primal urge switch straight over to full-on no holds barred. She moaned and his tongue traced along the top of her teeth, thrust greedily inside her mouth until it hit her own, and then he was circling, sucking and she opened her mouth wider, wanting more, greedy.

To hell with him not wanting her to touch, her fingers automatically wound their way into his forest of hair so that she could pull him closer, her body lifted to meet his.

Shit. She dragged her mouth away from his. 'What the…' A warm, dampness spread over her hand, more slobber than sex.

'Did we forget about you Sparks?' The horse threw its head up in alarm as she flung her arms in all directions and his soothing voice was all for the animal. Blast.

Why the hell, just when he'd stopped acting like an expert in self-defence had that happened? Thanks, horse, you offered me the chance and now you've taken it away. She shut her eyes.

He laughed. 'Don't move, I'll be back.'

Promising.

He murmured softly to the horse and she could hear him messing with tack, gathering things up.

'Can we just forget all the deep stuff for a bit?' *Move on to the mindless.*

He grinned and put out a hand, hauling her to her feet, but when she was up, there was only a sliver of air between their bodies, her breasts brushing lightly against him each time she took a breath. She was tempted to keep taking bigger breaths, but that would look a bit obvious.

'You believe all that garbage then? Can't people just get on and enjoy it?'

'Right now, I believe you talk too much. Aren't you ever quiet?' He put a finger on her lips. 'You need to open your mind, not your mouth.' His grin was lopsided. Cute. Not a word she'd thought she'd ever associate with him.

'Open mouth can be good.'

He shook his head. 'You're impossible.' Sliding his hand behind her head, his fingers threaded through her hair. A hand that slowly drifted down, tugging as it went, sending a shiver between her shoulder blades.

47

'You're good at this.' She dampened her dry lips, do or die. Just say it. 'I do want you.'

'I know.' The hoarse edge to his voice made her sway towards him.

'But, I'm not sure if what you're offering is good for me.' In fact she knew it wasn't. He was a walking disaster zone. She'd been lonely before. She was sure that he'd leave her a zillion times worse off.

'I'm not offering anything.' He lifted his hand again, did that running his fingers through the length of her hair thing that was almost hypnotic.

'Exactly.' She swallowed.

'So, do you want to do a disappearing act now, before I forget to give you the option?'

'No.' She bit her lip. She'd wanted more than Simon could have given her, she'd wanted passion and something more that had always been just out of reach, something she couldn't stick a label on. 'I don't want an option.'

'I can't give you what you're looking for.'

'I can't give *you* what you're looking for, if it involves total surrender.'

'You won't know till you try.' He laughed. 'And you're already part-way there.'

She was about to say 'what the hell is that supposed to mean?', but she couldn't because he kissed her again.

If she couldn't have anything else of him, that kiss was a bloody good thing to be going on with. Along with the way he was touching her, sending a tingle right down to the very bottom of her spine. As in, right down, way past her tail bone.

'Good?' He pulled away slightly, just so that she could see the serious expression on his face, feel his warm breath against her skin.

Good? It was chocolate and wine and cuddles and sex all wrapped up in one. His fingers carried on doing whatever they were doing on her waist, and the rest of her just carried on to slowly melt, or was that disintegrate? She nodded, swallowed hard again. Hard teeth tugged gently at her earlobe, and she tilted her head.

'What do you want?'

'Kiss my neck, please.' She sounded a bit like a strangled kitten but it didn't matter. He kissed, he sucked and her knees damned near gave way as pure want snaked its way between her thighs.

'Have you ever come when someone did this?' The damp heat of his tongue swept up to her ear. 'Have you ever fantasised about two men?' His other hand cradled her breast. 'Well?' Firm fingers squeezed her hardening nipple. Men weren't supposed to talk, they were just supposed to do.

What was the question? 'One man's enough.' *And right now, you're the one.* The palm of his hand over her breast was burning through her top, heating her skin.

'What if one man can't give you everything you want?'

'I'll change what I want.' She gasped as he sucked hard just where her neck met her shoulder. And as he did it he pulled her body tightly against his so that the ache between her legs was cradled against his erection. He held her firmly, one hand hard against her bum, his long fingers resting between her buttocks and as he held her tightly, his cock against her, she came.

A gentle, throbbing pulse that let her go. Released the tension, the want. 'One man deep inside you, the other kissing.' He bit gently along her shoulder. 'Sucking, kissing as you come.' She rocked against him, waiting for the feeling to fizzle out, then opened her eyes and she was looking straight into his black-violet ones.

'What are you hiding from?'

Her voice was soft and her eyes wide open. He gently eased his grip on her. 'I'm not hiding. I told you, I just don't want to get involved. I can't give you what you want.'

'And what do I want?'

'More than just good sex.'

'No, you're wrong, buster. Right now I want a good, hard shag,

I don't want to think about it, or talk about it. I want you to blow my mind, not bloody open it.'

'You already are open, Kez.' And she was. She was the complete opposite of him; she was standing like some tiny, defiant devil pulsing with need and yet she was open to suggestion, open to giving, to taking.

'Well, shag me then.' Her voice was a tiny whisper that ran along his spine right to the base, until it splintered out, making him hard. She seemed to know not to reach out, not to touch him.

'What do you fantasise about, Kez? Not two men?'

She shook her head and looked at him like he was mad, but didn't move. 'No, I told you. I want one man,' she hesitated, 'who I want so much I don't need anyone else.' A blush of pink had edged its way along her cheekbones and suddenly she wasn't a devil, she was more a fallen angel who had nothing to lose. 'Even if it's just for that moment.'

'One man who will do everything you ask him to?'

'No.' She licked her bottom lip nervously but her gaze didn't waver from his. 'I want him to take control.'

'To do what he wants to you?' His balls were tingling, stirring with the kind of need he usually reserved for the dreams that crept up on him. Nightmares that turned him on and frightened him off.

'No.' She swayed slightly. 'I want someone who will do what he knows I want him to.'

'A mind-reader.'

'You know what I want. I open my mind, you open yours.'

'You want me to pin you down.' This wasn't going the way it was supposed to. But he wasn't sure he cared. He wanted her in a way he couldn't remember wanting a woman in a long time, he wanted to please her. He wanted to fuck her. 'Hold you down so you can't say no.' His cock burned against his groin, he could feel the dampness of pre-come that made him want her more. 'Hold your legs open as I explore you inside, and you can't move, can't stop the sensations.' Her throat gave a tremor as she swallowed, her lips gently parted, waiting. 'You want to be turned on until you're begging for me to fuck you, but I don't.' She never moved as he stepped around her, stood behind her so that he could kiss her neck, shoulder, let the sweet smell of her sex grab at him even more. He nipped at the delicate skin with his teeth and she whimpered. He couldn't stand much more of this, he really did need to push his way inside that soft body. 'You want me to play with you, finger you inside until you want to clutch at me with your thighs, make yourself come, but I don't let you. I hold your legs wide, force you to let it build, force your body to let go.'

'Just fucking do it.' She spun round, went up on tiptoe, her body trembling with tension against his and reached up to kiss him. But he beat her to it. His mouth was crushing her soft lips, bruising, needing as his teeth skated along the edge of her tongue. She pulled away, panting. 'What do *you* want, James?'

She'd not used his name before, it was soft but with an intensity that hit him head-on. 'I want you to be mine, totally mine, just for this moment.' He'd spoken without thinking, she'd caught him off guard. But he'd spoken the truth. He did, and then after? He didn't want anyone to be his. She stripped her t-shirt over her head, the scarlet bra at odds with what he'd expected. 'Take your jeans and boots off.' She did, slowly. Totally unselfconsciously. He pushed her back against the wall. No more talking. No more thinking. Just their two bodies and what they needed. She trembled as her back hit the cold concrete. He nudged her legs apart with his knee and all he could see was the dark lust in her eyes, the challenge, the need. When his hand slipped into her knickers and met the damp warmth his throat dried, tightened. She was soaked, her panties were soaked from earlier, from now. He pushed two fingers into her slick channel and she sank down on to his hand, urged him deeper. He curled, found the uneven surface he was looking for and stroked. Her eyes widened, lips parted in invitation and he took her lower lip between his teeth, sucked it into his mouth as his fingers played against her g-spot. She was panting, her body flushing, the muscles in her thighs tightening as he knew they would. He pressed his knee against hers, forced her legs wider, made her accept the slow tease that he knew was building. The orgasm he knew he could give her if she'd let him. He rubbed harder against the swollen spot, resting his thumb against her clit gently, felt her pussy walls tighten around him. 'Relax, open.' He spoke straight into her mouth, nibbled the sweetness of her lip then sucked it gently back into his mouth as if he was sucking her swollen nub. She moaned, his stomach tightened as hers relaxed, as she did what he'd told her to and opened her core, open, open, and then she came in a rush, sweet juices flooded over his fingers and her pussy was contracting in surges that clutched at his hand. Shit, he couldn't wait any longer. He had his jeans unzipped as he was sliding his fingers out from her, had his cock nudging against her entrance whilst she was still trembling. And the smell of her juices on his hand, her flushed face as she gazed, shocked at him, almost tipped him over the edge. He gritted his teeth and thrust inside her so hard her body seemed to jolt as she clutched at his shoulders. Her nails were raking his skin, her teeth breaking the skin of his lips as he pulled out, thrust again. And her legs were wrapped around him, her body bouncing against him as he pushed deeper inside her, not able to stop, not able to hold himself back, just giving them both what they wanted.

She was trembling, digging her heels into his back, crying out, and he just hung onto her hips, held her tight so that he could drive on, so he could feel her come, then get there himself. Hard teeth were in his shoulder, she was tilting her hips, tipping closer, grinding against him and then he could feel her muscles gripping his cock, feel her thighs trembling against him and he lost it. Forcing her down harder against his groin, he tightened his thigh muscles until they burned as he emptied himself into her.

'Fuck.' He put one hand out onto the wall to steady himself. It had obviously been far, far too long since he'd had a no-holds-barred shag. His whole body was shaking and for a second he felt light-headed. He shook himself. Looked blankly at her.

She smiled. 'Way to go.' Slowly untangling her limbs from his, she stood up. 'Thanks for letting me in.' Then she ran cool fingers down his cheek, kissed him with a barely there touch on the lips and bent down to pick up her clothes.

He watched, slightly dazed as she sauntered across the arena, stark naked, clothes dangling from her hand, her neatly rounded butt swaying slightly as she went. And she didn't look back. Just kept going. Lifting one hand in a half wave as she went.

And he wondered what the fuck he'd just done.

# Chapter 5

'Don't you go shopping then?'

'Not really.' He'd untacked Sparky and turned him out, and then headed off to find her, because he had been intrigued at what she was going to do next. Which, it appeared, involved making lunch.

'All I could find was baked beans.'

'Nothing wrong with beans on toast.' He pulled out a chair.

'A bit farty isn't it if you don't eat anything else?'

'You're funny.'

'Says he.' She stabbed the beans with her fork. 'I've been thinking.'

'Sounds dangerous.'

She frowned. 'I don't think I have a problem with surrendering, it just comes naturally, whereas you-' A fork was waved in his direction, but she didn't add anything.

'Hmm, I don't think you have any problem at all.' He took a mouthful of the food and wondered where she was going with this and at what point he should head her off. 'You're just so easy.'

She grinned and gave a little shrug. 'Well, maybe I turn into a pushover if there's a hot stud in the room.' He'd never met anyone quite so open, well not since he'd passed puberty. Open, unaffected, non-judgemental. 'But you do have a problem.' She stabbed the fork in his direction again. Nosy. Then went back to the beans.

54

'Must admit it turned me on, though, you talking about fantasies.'

'Just offering possibilities.'

'You're going pompous again.' He couldn't help but smile. Miss Plain Talking, Miss Pain in the Ass. 'But I guess no one has ever asked me that kind of stuff before, so I never told them.' She stirred the beans round absent-mindedly. 'What were you thinking about when you were pounding away?'

He looked straight back into that steady gaze and wanted to be honest. 'Making you come, letting go.' He paused. 'I wanted to shag you senseless, Kez. I wanted to forget everything else and bury myself in you and hammer away until it all exploded.'

'It certainly did that.' She put the fork down, which was lucky for the beans and the toast. 'Why did you leave your old life?'

'I hated the people.' It had all been pretence, everyone looking after themselves, everyone competing to be the best.

'But you had everything, I don't understand. I mean what about your family? Your wife?'

'Family?' He studied his plate for a moment, then looked back up at her. 'Family isn't everything, Kez. Family ties you down and makes you play the game.' Family was why he'd tried to stay, why he'd let Chloe slowly shred him up. Family were the ones who would despise him if they ever understood what she'd done, what he'd let her do.

'Family are important.' Her voice was small, and her defiance seemed to have melted away, but he ignored it.

'Bollocks. All that family, security, education, shit that you think is important. It's all just smoke and mirrors.'

Her hand was trembling, a slow shake against the plate that was making an irritating noise.

'You had it all and you just threw it away.'

'What kind of an idiot wants it all?' He forced himself to lower his voice, but he could hear the bitter edge. 'Who wants to slot the important things into windows in their fucking diary?'

'I do. I'm the kind of idiot who wants to understand long words, who wants a fucking diary to fill up.'

'Well I feel sorry for you. Do you really want to schedule in sex night? Be sucking a guy off under the dinner table because you're bored out of your brain with talking politics?'

'You didn't?' For a moment she perked up.

'Not me personally.' He gave the closest he could to a smile and felt some of the tension ease out of him. He shouldn't let it get to him. Not now, not any more.

'I'm the kind of idiot who wants my family back, James, the kind of idiot who wants a guy and I don't think I'm the one who's got it wrong. You're the one who's running away and I haven't got a clue why, but just because you've given up on it, doesn't make it all wrong.' She stood up, her chair legs screeching against the hard floor. 'And if you don't let someone in to that stupid head of yours one day soon you'll drive yourself nuts.'

He pushed his own chair back. It was her who would drive him nuts if he listened to any more of this drivel. He didn't have to listen to lectures from a naïve girl who'd never known anything but flaming love and freedom.

'And you'll drive everyone else nuts as well.' She had her hands on those slim little hips and was looking at him like she expected a response. Well, sod that. What was it with women? One shag and they thought they have a right to your thoughts. James felt his mouth tighten as he gave her one last look, then spun around, his fists clenched at his sides as he stormed out of the house.

Kezia watched him as he headed off across the yard. What did they say? Mean, moody and magnificent? Well you could just stick with the mean as far as he went. Talk about still waters running deep. James was deep enough to drown himself and everyone else. Underneath it all he was just about to explode into something as turbulent as a bloody tsunami. She glanced back at the half-full plates, wishing there was a dog to feed the scraps to, looked back again and he'd disappeared. Bloody Houdini.

She guessed he'd lost control a bit when they'd been at it; she'd certainly lost it. She'd wanted him so fiercely she would have done anything to make sure he stayed there. And he'd wanted it, but she wasn't quite sure what. She wasn't sure if he was letting out some frustration he'd been trying to bury, or whether he was letting out the real him. There was always a chance, she supposed, that he'd been thinking about someone else; whoever it was he'd surrendered to once upon a time. Yeah, he'd been in love once, she was sure of that. And he was making damned sure he didn't do it again. He was scary when he got so intense and wound up.

She scraped the food off the plates and dropped it in the bin. And now he was running again. She sighed. She would give anything to have all the things he was so intent on throwing away. Anything and everything to have a family. And there was too much of a nice side to him to believe he meant what he said. Well, he meant it, but did he really believe it? She wiped her hands down her jeans. She had to put up with him for the rest of the summer and he had to put up with her. She knew she wasn't easy, she knew she could be a pain in the neck and she knew she talked too much, but at least she was pleasant and he could be too. He just had to be told.

She pulled her boots back on and headed out of the front door with her mobile vibrating ten to the dozen in the pocket of her tight jeans. She knew exactly who that would be. The one person who did actually want to be in the same room as her. What was it Simon's last text had said? 'If you won't talk to me on the phone, guess I might have to come and find you'. He was mad. They were all mad. Now, where the fuck would James have gone off on his high horse?

It was the horses that pointed her in the right direction. They'd all gathered at the far corner of the field, which meant they'd followed him there. Horses liked James, James liked horses. James liked everything except her, or maybe it was women in general. But he liked Marie. She could tell by the way Marie had talked about him that they were close. Best thing since sliced bread, according to the woman that Kezia had trusted with her future. Well, trusted enough to pack her rucksack and head back to team GB. Well he was bloody mouldy sliced bread as far as she was concerned.

She realised she was slightly out of breath as she clambered over the fence, so she sat on the top for a moment for a breather. Why the hell was she rushing, he wasn't exactly going to go anywhere was he? No, he wanted her to go. Off his farm and leave the grumpy bastard on his own. Which was mildly tempting, apart from the issue of no money, no job and nowhere to stay. She kind of liked it here anyway. She liked the peace and quiet, and she even liked him, in a strange way. He had a magnetic attraction. It was a shame that from his side it was a magnetic repulsion. Hmm, well he wasn't exactly repulsed by her. He was more like a wild cat, who'd only let you go so far with the petting before he decided you were lunch. Or not even worth a nibble.

She was losing it, going mad.

Well, fine if he didn't really like her, he was stuck with her and she would give it one last chance at trying to get him to hide his nasty side, and then she'd play him at his own game.

When she slipped off the fence it was onto longer grass, where it hadn't been grazed and it was obvious where he'd walked. A small path led down a bank through a few trees and to a river. Wow. For a moment she forgot why she was there.

The trees had parted, opened out into a small glade and stream that bubbled gently by. It was the perfect spot.

At first she didn't spot him. He was motionless, stretched out, still, like a hare hiding out and waiting for the hounds to pass by. But the glint of his buckle caught her eye. He had his eyes shut, but she knew he was aware of her.

'Are you even breathing?'

He grunted, so she nudged him with her toe.

'You're enough to wake the dead crashing through the

undergrowth.'

She wasn't. She was about to say so, then remembered she was supposed to be conciliatory. Peace mission.

'You don't want me here do you?' She sat down. 'But I'm staying.' Just so he knew there was no question on that one. 'How can you be all wonderful one minute, then a complete wuss in a parade the next?'

'Interesting turn of phrase.' He didn't look at her, just lay there, but at least he hadn't told her to sod off. 'You got on with your parents I take it? What happened?'

'Can we leave that bit for now?' He'd wound her up, struck at the things she most valued and she just knew that if she started talking about what happened to them now it would end in tears. Literally. 'But I did get on with them, yeah.' She crossed her legs and stared down at the water. 'We did everything together, that's what happens when you're always on the move and an only child. They understood whatever I did, sometimes maybe too much.'

'Always reasonable and could see your side of things?' He glanced briefly in her direction and then back away.

'Mm. Nice spot you've got here.'

'Yup, I come here for—'

'Let me guess, peace and quiet.'

'You got it.'

'The only thing they couldn't give me was permanence, and I only realised I needed it after they'd gone.'

'No one can give you permanence, Kez. It's an illusion.' At least he didn't sound bitter now, just like he accepted it. Totally.

'I can.' She picked at a blade of grass next to her, splitting it down the middle. 'I can find me a place to stay.'

'It won't make you happy.'

'It might.' For now. 'And if it doesn't I can always try again.'

'I always lived in the same place, same house, brother, sister, dog, you name it. But we could have all been on different planets. Dad was, is, a barrister, Mum was on every committee going and we were supposed to be independent and competitive. Everything was done to a timetable, including what we talked about at dinner.' He gave a wry smile.

'But they loved you?'

'Who knows? They were busy, far too busy for kids. We had a nanny when we were young, then were expected to suddenly be transformed into adults.'

'So you weren't close, but I'm sure they did love you.'

'They could be proud, give the pat on the head when they thought we deserved it, so whichever of us had a bad week would be jealous of the one that got the attention.'

'But you were fine? And you did well. They must have been proud of what you did.'

'They were, I got the obligatory first at uni and then the city job, so I got my pat on the head. But,' he put his hands under his head, 'was I motivated to do my best to please them, or to please me?'

'A bit of both?' She stretched her legs out as cramp started to prickle.

'I wanted a lot more than to just be like them. Once I realised I was running uphill for someone else I started to backslide, I realised it was all crap, but coming here made me feel better about myself. I can be who I want.'

'But you're still hiding.'

He laughed, a low chuckle, then he rolled onto his side, propped himself up on one elbow and studied her. Slowly. From the top of her head all the way down to the soles of her feet.

'It's rude to stare.' She could feel herself start to tingle all over when he did that.

'I was trying to work out what the hell I did to deserve you dropping in. I must have been so bad in a past life.' He grinned.

'You're very lucky to have me here.' She nodded, trying to keep a straight face. 'And don't you forget it.'

'I'm sure you'll keep reminding me.' He gave a long drawn-out sigh that seemed to be resignation rather than frustration. And not aimed at her.

'So, why did you get married?' Strike while the iron is hot. He was talking, so why stop now? Her mum always said she never knew when to give up, which was more of a criticism than in her favour, she suspected.

'You ever thought of joining MI5, or the KGB?'

'Naw, I'm only interested in interrogating hot men. So?'

'The normal.' His voice was a low, sexy drawl and he was still watching her. Maybe he was going to pounce when he got fed up of talking. Well, she could live in hope. 'Met a girl, fell in lust.'

'You fell in love, admit it.'

He shook his head slowly at her. 'At the time it might have felt like it. Another time, eh?' He rolled back over, which meant the conversation was over.

'James?'

'Just lie down, shut up and—'

'Think of England?'

'Very droll. Listen.'

'To what?'

'You won't know until you try it.'

'And if—'

'Kez, if you don't shut up I will gag you and tie you up, and believe me it won't be sexually motivated.'

'It might not start off that way…' She smiled to herself, lay back like he'd told her and closed her eyes. She'd done lots of lying back and listening to nothing in her time. But only when she was on her own, she'd never shared it and she guessed he probably hadn't either. It was a bit, well, weird. Like you were waiting for something to happen.

She shifted uneasily and his hand came over hers and stayed there. For the first time since she'd arrived back in the UK she relaxed. Someone had taken hold of her, someone would look out for her.

There were fire engines, sirens, lights that flashed until all she could see was the glare. A crowd of people staring, blocking her way. But she knew she had to get past them, knew she had to see what was going on.

She fought her way through the crowd, pushed closer to the flashing lights, the heat that rolled its way out from some hell-like centre. And then she saw it, the car. Flames licking over the windows, red-orange flames flicking up at the windscreen. There was a shatter of glass, a piercing noise that broke the eerie silence, a shocked gasp and then the smell; acrid smoke and burning rubber. Particles of dust, burnt remnants that the breeze caught up and tossed into the air, swirling, lifting out of her reach. And on the smoke-blackened windows, all that remained were the streaks of darkening crimson, a weird mix of ochre and scarlet, drops that hung, suspended forever, smears that forced their way down. Blood.

They wouldn't let her past. They stopped her, dragged her back as she struck out. Pinned her arms to her sides and held her so that she couldn't move. But she could see. A black cloud that belched out as water fought fire. And all she could do was scream, a silent scream that nobody heard. That nobody listened to. And still the flames licked their way to destruction, ate up everything in their path, slowly swallowed up her life.

'Hey.'

She glanced up. But it wasn't a firefighter. It was him. James, materialising in front of her like some ghost on silent footsteps.

'Are you okay?'

A cold, clammy hand seemed to have taken hold of her, a noise hammered in her head and the pain in her chest hurt; it hurt so much.

There was a snap of fire and she jumped to her feet.

'Steady.'

It wasn't fire, there was no heat. No sound. She glanced around wildly. No fire, where was the fire? Dizziness wrapped around her and everything moved, the whole world tilted, then edged slowly back as he pulled her against him.

'It's okay.' She licked her dry lips and wondered why her voice sounded so strange. 'I'm fine. I got up too quickly. What's that noise?' It was wrong, sirens here in the middle of nowhere, but now they'd stopped.

'I'd just got up to see, climbed up onto the bank, and then you screamed.' He looked worried, stepped back slightly and she heard the crackle, the snap again.

She glanced down. Twigs, just dry twigs cracking under his feet. She closed her eyes briefly and tried to stop the trembling that had started to thread its way through her body. It was always like this, but she could control it, could stop it.

'I don't scream.'

He was giving her a look that said she did. 'No fire engines up at the house, though I did wonder if it could have anything to do with your baked beans.'

'Fire engine. Oh shit, the house is on fire!' The irrational fear kicked in again, the one she couldn't shake. 'What if someone's trapped and it's my fault?' She pulled away, or at least tried to, but he didn't let go. 'We have to—'

'There's no one there Kez. Steady on. It's just us; everyone else is away.'

'But—'

'I said there isn't a fire engine.' He spoke slowly, as if she was stupid. 'And I couldn't see any flames or even smoke, just a fire engine going somewhere else.'

'What if there is a fire?' The rapid banging in her chest was slowing.

'There isn't.' The pressure of his fingers increased on her arms. 'They probably stopped here to check which house it was. The farms around here are pretty spread out.'

'But—'

'Stop saying "but". Come on, I think you need to sit down somewhere warm.' He took a firm grip on her hand. 'You okay

63

to walk up to the house?'

'I'm fine.' She took a deep breath, trying to drag herself back to normality, stared at their linked hands. 'What's that for?'

'So you don't rush off and fall in a ditch or something.'

'Huh.'

He was right. As they got closer to the house she could see that for herself. No fire, no flames. And as they walked slowly in, still holding hands, no wall of heat met them. Not even burned toast or baked beans.

But she was still shaking inside, and she could taste the tang of smoke, even though it wasn't there to taste. She swallowed down hard, forcing the unexpected taste of bile away, and hoped she'd plastered a smile, not a grimace, to her face. She wiggled her fingers to prove to herself that she didn't need to hang on to his hand.

'You can let go now.' He didn't.

'Not until you stop trembling and looking like you might keel over.'

'I can't put the kettle on if you don't.' She needed to do something normal, needed to make a drink, even if she knew she probably wouldn't be able to drink it. Her stomach was still churning uneasily, her skin prickling with a cold dampness that normally woke her up in the night, when thoughts crept up on her and she was powerless to stop them. When she lay awake waiting for them to hunt her down, to find her. When the flames that flickered would be just for her. The stab of unease twisted a little deeper in her chest. She was being stupid, irrational. She was fine here. She was safe. .

'Look I don't want to leave you, but I need to do the horses.'

'I'll help.' Staying on her own would make it worse. Doing something normal would chase the demons away.

'You can stay here and have that coffee.'

'I'll help.'

He sighed.

'It's what Marie's paying me for.' *And partly why I packed my stuff and travelled back to a country I hardly remember.*

'You're a stubborn cow.'

He stepped closer, took her chin between firm fingers and looked into her eyes. His own looked violet in this light; a strange reflective hue, like the sky at midnight. Unearthly. She let herself just stand and look back at him. She could lose herself in a man like him. Something deep inside of her was drawn to him, trusted him and right now she couldn't be bothered to fight it. She wanted someone to hang on to, even if one day soon he'd slip through her fingers like the mercurial devil that he was. He'd be gone, scared of being trapped by someone who needed him.

'Stubborn as a mule, and I prefer mule to cow.'

The corner of his mouth twitched. She liked it when she did that to him.

'Okay, but if you collapse in a heap don't blame me. You look rough.'

'Thanks.' She felt rough. Like she'd been run over by a bulldozer. He didn't grab her hand again, though, and he left her to it once he was sure she knew what she was doing. They were both sorting their own block of stables, bringing the horses in, feeding them.

'You don't have to check I've done them all properly, you know.'

'I wasn't.' He grinned.

But she'd watched as he'd looked over the whole yard with his eagle eye. 'You were, you liar. I do know how to shut a stable door.' She supposed he could have said that she should know how to avoid burning toast. But he didn't. Instead he headed back to the house and she followed, feeling more tired than she had in a long time.

By the time she'd showered she could smell the food. After she'd changed and gone downstairs again there was a spaghetti bolognese on the table and an open bottle of red wine, which she hoped didn't mean he wanted to start talking.

'So, we've called a truce?'

'As long as you promise not to do the cooking or talk too much.'

He held out a glass to her, the heat of his fingertips brushing against hers as she took it. And he looked far more dangerously sexy than any man she'd met in her entire life.

He regretted the wisecrack as soon as it slipped out of his mouth. She was tired, totally knackered and still washed-out and pale. He'd not seen her like this since he'd found her landed on the gate. He let her eat, let her sip the wine, let the warmth seep into her and the words come back. He watched her mouth move as she talked, her generous mouth animated. He didn't listen, just watched and heard the intonation, heard the confidence come back.

'What was all that about, then?'

She put the fork down carefully, so that it barely made a noise. She shifted uneasily on her seat. For a moment it looked as though she wasn't going to talk; he could see the internal battle running across her features. The fight to be open warring against the fear of reliving whatever it was that hurt so much. Then she fixed him with a look he hadn't seen from her before; hurt eyes that looked almost empty. A shiver of unease ran down his spine. Kezia never looked blank. She was always alive, her eyes dancing with the bubbling life within. She stared for a long moment, but he knew she wasn't seeing him.

'When they managed to put the fire out they were burned beyond recognition. They wouldn't let me see them – just gave me their wedding rings and said dental records had confirmed their identities.'

'Who?'

'Mum and Dad.' Her voice was oddly steady. 'It had melted them away, taken their skin and hair.'

'Kez?'

She focused back on him.

'They wouldn't let me near the car, but I knew it was theirs, ours. They held me back and it was still burning. I'd only been standing there a few seconds when the windscreen shattered. It was like a bomb had gone off.' There was an edge of wonderment to her voice that unnerved him.

'They were in an accident?'

'No.' She frowned at him as though he was being stupid. 'Oh, no, they were already dead. They killed them.' She was still frowning, as though trying to work something out. Her voice was so matter-of-fact. 'The police agreed the car had been set alight so that no one would know, to destroy the evidence.' She looked at him. 'But we did know. It was the blood.' Her eyes cleared and as they did the tears built. 'There was still blood everywhere.' Her lower lip trembled, and the sudden urge to hold her almost caught him unawares. Her eyes were brimming full, overflowing, one single tear traced its way down her cheek. And it hurt him more than if she'd broken down.

He moved round, pulled her close before he had time to think about it.

'I can't, I don't want to...'

'Shh. Don't say anything else.' Her slim body was shaking against his. He'd spent the afternoon slagging off his family, scoffing at her need for security and she'd let him, let him mouth off like an idiot. And she'd called herself the stupid one. She'd gone from having a closeness he could only guess at, to being all alone. And he'd never once seen her drop her guard and feel sorry for herself. And Marie must have known. Anger surged through his body. Why hadn't she warned him? He forced himself to relax. He'd been the one to say he didn't look after waifs and strays.

She was close against his body, swaying slightly against him, not clinging on but just holding. All the energy seemed to have drained from her and he didn't know how to give it back.

She barely made a noise as he swung her up into his arms. She was so light, she didn't seem to be the same girl that he'd had in his arms earlier in the day. She never moved a muscle as he made his way up the stairs. Never spoke or made the slightest sign that she knew he was there.

He laid her gently down on the bed and she just looked at him through bleary eyes, her face tear-stained, and then rolled over, curled up on her side.

Pulling the cover over her, he gently tucked it around her and she didn't move. She just closed her eyes, rested her face on one hand and her breathing settled.

He watched for a minute, then moved silently out of the room, went down to the kitchen and poured himself a glass of wine.

Open your mind he'd said. What a joke. She'd responded to everything he'd said, everything he'd done and he'd still not known a thing about her. He'd been making a point about sex and completely missing the point about her life. She'd allowed him into her mind, but only to the tiny part of her that was lust and need; the sexual part of her that he'd thought was all he wanted to know. And he'd just discovered it wasn't.

He'd been right to be determined to keep away from her, but for her sake not his.

He emptied the last drops of wine from the bottle into his half-empty glass, slowly put the bottle back down and swilled the liquid around in his glass. What had she meant when she said 'the police had agreed'? Why had she been so sure that they'd been killed, sure enough to spot the blood, sure enough to be frightened?

## Chapter 6

'Teach me something.' She was peering over her coffee cup, with eyes that had bruised circles under them, but the smile that played on her lips was natural. 'I want to be useful.'

'What do you want to learn, oh eager one?' He stirred his coffee, unable to help but smile back.

'Horse stuff. Right,' she pushed her cup to one side and leaned forward slightly, 'when you talk to them they just settle down and do stuff, move over or whatever, but they ignore me.' She was obviously on a mission, had decided her plan for the day and no one was going to get in the way. Least of all him.

'They don't know you.'

'Or they leap away.'

'You move too fast, that's scary for herbivores.'

'And I want to be able to ride like you do. You just sit there and do nothing.' She glared at him accusingly. 'And I can be kicking like hell or hauling on the reins.'

He laughed. 'Ever heard of one step at a time?'

She looked at him suspiciously. 'You're not going back to that close-your-eyes crap?'

'Everything you don't understand is crap, isn't it?'

'Well you know what I mean.' Back to the defensive look. 'I want to get on with it, and I can do it.'

'You can, it's not complicated. But—'

'Here we go, but this, but that.'

'If you give me a chance.' He put a finger over her lips to stop her talking. She'd drive him round the bend if he let her. 'You can learn anything, but only when you're ready for it. Yeah, you go jump on a horse and gallop around and tell everyone you can ride, but if you want that horse to work with you then you need to become part of it, not just perch on the top. You can't ride if you're scared.'

'I'm not scared.'

He put his whole hand over her mouth and her eyes widened. Then her tongue snaked out against his palm, cheekily. He'd be fine as long as her teeth didn't join in, then he'd be in trouble. Then they'd be in this kitchen for quite a bit longer. He tried not to think about pushing her over the large pine table.

'Horses are sensitive. They know if you want to be there with them, or if you're just passing the time of day. You really tune into that animal and all you have to do is think and it will go how you want.'

She bit his palm, and not in a sexy way, so he gave up on trying to keep her quiet. 'Yeah, think. Sure.'

'You think about turning left and you automatically move that way, with your head if nothing else; the horse senses it and goes with you. Simple as that – nothing weird or wonderful. But if you're kicking away and waving your arms, how the hell can it hear what you really want?'

'Do you know what I really want?'

'Nope, but I'm pretty sure you're going to tell me.'

'Nasty. Well, I'm not. You'll have to tune in.' She grinned and jumped up. 'Come on, grumpy, come and teach me horse stuff or I'll have to close my eyes and work it out on my own.'

Whatever had happened to his summer of peace? To doing all the jobs around the place that needed doing? To having time on his own?

'If you don't teach me horse stuff,' she paused, hand on the door jamb, waiting for him, 'I'll have to consider the sex stuff.' She giggled. 'I could tell them exactly how to get laid.'

'God help us.'

He rolled his eyes as she stroked a hand slowly down her body and pouted suggestively. 'You going to come and sort me out, then?'

There was an answer to that. The stirrings in his groin were telling him that sorting her out would be far from unpleasant. And then what?

'I think you're short of a good spanking.'

'Now, there's a new one.'

'But for now I'll settle for getting you on a horse if it'll stop you pestering.'

She smiled back at him, a full-blown happy smile that stirred him far more than it should be doing. 'Don't we need to muck out first?'

'I did that while you were still snoring.' He'd wanted to let her get some rest. Yesterday she'd scared him, no one should look so drained, exhausted. And he'd been afraid to go and wake her, afraid of what he'd do if she reached for him. Afraid that seeing her vulnerable would drag him in deeper, that he'd start caring even more. He mentally kicked himself. Yeah, *more* was the problem because he did already care. And he still wasn't really sure he wanted to.

She frowned. 'But, I still get paid, right? It's not my fault you did it early.'

'Not my fault you can't get up in the mornings.'

'This place needs a dog you know, you need a dog.' He was getting used to the sudden changes in conversation, he dreaded to think what the inside of her mind looked like.

'I haven't got time for a dog.'

'It would be good for you, give you something to cuddle.'

He raised an eyebrow. 'Do I honestly look like I need something to cuddle?'

71

'Well, to be honest, you look like you need a woman to cuddle not a dog, but you keep saying you don't want one of those.'

'Kez?'

'Yep?'

'Shut up and get that pert little arse down to the stables before I give in to temptation and spank it.'

'Yes, sir.' She grinned and scarpered. He stood, pushed his chair slowly in and adjusted his jeans. Joking around with a woman wasn't supposed to turn him on, but it was with her. You could lie in bed and joke with a woman like Kez. Laugh and share. He put his palm on his forehead, shut his eyes and slid it down until he had finger and thumb either side of his chin and then he shook his head. It didn't help solve the problem at all.

She was pretty sure her mobile would go into meltdown if she didn't answer this call. All she had to do was answer it once, just once; it wouldn't encourage him, it would just make things clear. And then the endless calls and texts would stop. She crossed her fingers behind her back and pressed the answer call button.

'Kez?'

'Hi Simon.'

'Where've you been? You haven't rung, I didn't know if you'd even got there okay.' There was touch of the petulant boy lurking in his voice. *Whatever happened to 'hello, how are you?'* 'You said you'd call.'

'Sorry, Si.' She resisted the urge to sigh. She had to be nice, she'd left him. But, that was the point. She'd left because it was never going to work. And she hadn't said she'd call, because you didn't do that when you left someone, did you?

'So, have you decided how long you're going to stay there? I miss you.'

What was she supposed to do, tell him she'd missed him too and let him think there was a chance? Cruel to be kind was the type of crap thing you only said when you didn't have to do it.

Nasty wasn't nice. 'I'm not sure yet. It's good. I like it.' James was watching her from across the yard. Still, staring, not looking happy.

'You met many people?'

*Just one.* 'Not many, I've only been here a few days.'

'Are they being nice to you?'

*Tricky one.* 'Yeah, sure, everyone's nice.' She shifted her weight to the other foot. 'I'm not coming back, Si.'

'You've met someone else.' He gave a short laugh, saying it but dismissing it.

'It's not that.' Although after sex with James, going back to a romp between the sheets with someone like Simon was going from steak to spam. Steak with sides, and relish and a dollop of spicy salsa on the top. She gave an inward sigh. She'd always been happy with spam before, what had got into her? Except just having James standing several yards away, emanating danger and thrills was enough to answer the question.

'You have, I can tell.' He huffed and puffed a bit, and she shuffled her feet in the dirt a bit more and wondered how to end the conversation. 'I'll still be here when you get fed up and want to come home.' And he clicked off. Which saved her doing it and stopped her being able to say again that it was over. This was probably why he'd cut her off, but at least he hadn't mentioned coming over. Finding her. She ran a finger over the screen. Was she ever going to find somewhere she could call home? Home is where the heart is, wasn't that what they said? Home had once been with Mum and Dad, but now?

She pushed away from the wall and shoved her mobile deep down into her pocket, headed towards James, who appeared to have come over all moody again now that she'd left him waiting.

'Here.' He held out a halter, keeping hold of it a second longer than he had to. 'Problem?'

She tugged it free of him. 'No, it was just a friend.'

'Boyfriend?'

Why did men always assume it was another man? 'Friend.' But

he'd narrowed his eyes a bit, bloody mind reader. 'Ex. Not that I can see it matters.'

'True.' He shrugged. 'You just seemed bothered, that's all.'

*Hmm and you just look bothered, mate.* She swung the halter in her hand. 'Lesson time, cowboy.'

'I hope I'm not going to regret this.' He gave a mock stern look as she linked her hand through his arm. 'Poor bloody horses.'

She was starting to see why Marie liked him. When he forgot about being stern and defensive he had this vibe that made you relax and feel safe, instantly. Which was probably what the horses responded to. Zero adrenalin. The trouble was that he kept mixing it with one hundred per cent danger where she was concerned and one minute her heart was beating slowly enough to send her into a cosy coma, then the next it was hammering like it wanted independence.

They walked over to the gate and he ushered her through, clicking the catch shut behind them. 'So, if you had a choice, which one would you go for?'

Several of the horses had lifted their heads, one large bay had ambled over and was resting its chin on James' shoulder, waiting for him to reassure it. Behind it a grey was muscling in.

Kezia looked, swinging the halter from side to side. The grey spooked and she glanced up to see a wry look from James. 'Be still. Can you do still?'

She could do still. Not that she could do it like him. 'You must have been an animal in a past life.'

'Concentrate Kez, just for two minutes, can you?'

'I like that one.' She'd watched the chestnut from her bedroom window. Its coat gleamed iridescent as the sun set. It was always the first to raise its head when there was a noise in the distance, and yet always the one that grazed peacefully as the others milled around. The one that did its own thing.

'This should be interesting.' He gave her what she guessed was a cynical smile. And a challenge. 'Go get him then, girl.'

'Is this a trick?'

'No trick.' He held his hands up. 'I'll catch Monty first. You watch, then do the same, okay?'

She'd seen Monty in action before. He was the one that galloped fastest, showed his teeth and heels most, and could be stubborn as a mule. He was the one that snorted at her when she fed him and looked like hurricane Harriet had hit if she waved the empty bucket within half a mile.

James walked steadily over, slipped the halter on and led the horse back, the lead rope slack in his hands. Monty widened his nostrils at Kez so she glared, so he stepped back in mock alarm. James put a hand on his neck, one stroke and his head dropped. Hmm, she knew how that felt. One stroke. 'Go get your victim then.' He gave a gentle laugh that she was sure had a hidden warning in there somewhere.

'What's he called?'

'Red.' He winked.

'Red? What kind of name is that?'

'I'll explain later. Go on.'

So she did. She got within ten yards and he did that head-in-the-air thing, but stood his ground. Five yards, four yards, then he turned and wheeled off, tail cocked high.

She glanced at James, who was lounging against the gate like he was expecting to be there for a while, Monty quietly grazing around his feet.

She tried soothing noises, not that she'd heard James actually doing them, but it worked in the movies. It made it worse. Horses scattering in all directions as the bugger flew straight at the rest of them on purpose. Any second now and it would turn into a rodeo.

'Okay, smart arse.' The darned horse had actually ended up right by the bloody gate, tossing his heels in James' direction, and then scarpered as she'd headed that way. She could have caught any bloody horse, but that one. 'You knew he'd do that didn't you?'

He shrugged.

'So, go on. You're the teacher; teach.'

'Are you ready to learn?' He eased away from the fence and he was looking serious, so she just nodded. Three times around the bloody field hadn't made her any wiser. 'Here.' He handed her Monty's lead rope. 'Watch.' She watched. She could come over all poetic watching him. He had an easy stride, not a jarring move in sight. And he was fit. Those leans legs and those broad shoulders that stretched his shirt to within an inch of its life just demanded attention. Even if he didn't want it. He held the halter easily, but the fact that his fingers were curled tightened the muscles in his forearms, forearms that had a smattering of hair that she wanted to touch.

He moved further away from her; five yards from Red, four. Bugger and blast, the damned horse was motionless, just watching him, like she was. He reached up, hooked under the noseband, and stroked a hand easily along the slightly sweated neck. Then he released him. And turned back to her. Took a couple of steps her way, stood with his hands on his hips. 'Were you watching closely?'

'I was.' She certainly was; every move of every muscle.

'Go ahead then.'

She tried to switch her brain out of lust mode and into concentration. She wasn't great at the whole thinking thing, but she was darned good at imitating people. It was how she'd always learned. Books didn't work for her, words got mixed up and confused things, but watching people do things? Well she had what was almost a photographic memory, for images, movements. So she copied. Not right down to the swaggering loping walk; no way could she do that. But she could do going in at angle, she could do keeping her head tilted down, which she guessed meant he wasn't glaring the animal out like she had; she could do standing side on and slipping the noseband up. She could do catching Red.

'Good.' His voice was soft, but the warmest she'd heard, not just from him, but from anyone in her whole life. It was a warm hand reaching out and curling around her. And when she looked up, because it was fine to look him in the eye even if horses weren't too keen, she guessed she'd done okay. He had an assessing look and something else that she couldn't pin down, but thought that it could be a thumbs up. She'd never been into feeling warm and fuzzy but it was one pretty good description for how she felt.

Then she fucked it up. She swung the end of the lead rope in self-congratulation and Red reared up. It hurt, it bloody felt like her arm had been pulled out of its socket. A searing pain brought tears to her eyes. She knelt down, hanging on to her arm, hearing the gallop of hooves as Red disappeared into the distance.

'What the fuck?' Low controlled anger, which was worse than being bawled at.

Honeymoon over, normal service resumed. And she felt sick.

'Are you going to go and get him?'

No would be the answer to that one. But she daren't open her mouth. She shook her head and bit down on her lip to try and hold it together. He gave a horse-like harrumph. Muttered something that didn't sound complimentary and sloped off.

She didn't hear him come back. The first she knew was when the warmth of his hand came down on her back, which made her jump, and made her shoulder hurt like hell. Again.

'You okay?'

*Nope.* When she didn't answer he squatted down beside her, put a hand on the arm she was clutching. 'Shit, I'm sorry.' God only knew why he was sorry. She felt dizzy, weird. 'I didn't realise…'

'You never stop to realise do you?' She was gritting her teeth and didn't even know if he could hear her, but it made her feel better saying it.

'No.'

The soft word made her look up, and he was there. Stooped down in front of her. Midnight eyes looking straight into her own. 'Maybe I don't. Here.' His fingers moved gently up her arm. 'Let me check your shoulder.' It couldn't hurt any more than it already did, so she let him. Closing her eyes, she realised she wasn't going to keel over and die imminently. 'No real damage done.'

'That's easy for you to say.'

'Sit down.' He pushed her back gently. 'I was afraid you'd dislocated it. Look,' his fingers gently probed around the socket, 'I meant it, I am sorry. You did well.'

'Until I cocked it up. Ouch, can you stop doing that now you've proved your point?'

'I was just scared he'd tangle the rope around his legs and come down from the speed he took off at. I just reacted and I shouldn't have.' He put a hand under her chin. Firm fingers lifting her face, his thumb traced down over her cheek, rubbing the damp tears into her skin.

'Sorry.' She was being nasty when he was trying to be nice.

'No, I'm the one who should be sorry. You did do a good job catching him, honestly. I don't say things unless I mean them.'

'Don't I know it.' He was one of those guys who never said sorry, one of those guys who never gave you a pat on the head like he'd said his Dad had been. Except she suspected he was nothing like his Dad really. It wasn't that he didn't want to get close, more that he wouldn't let himself. For whatever reason.

'It wound me up a bit, you and the boyfriend.' He sat down close, his hand still on her shoulder.

'On the phone? Really?' She forgot the 'ouch' factor for a moment, remembered Simon and felt guilty again. 'He is just a friend.'

'It's none of my business.'

'He's called Simon.' James' thigh pressed against hers was beginning to have an effect, even though the pressure was so slight. She could lean in a bit? *No, behave Kez.* 'We were dating, but it wasn't serious. Well, it looks now like he was serious but I didn't realise and I was—'

'Just enjoying the moment?'

'Something like that, I suppose. We got on fine, he was nice.' She shrugged. 'I thought we were on the same wavelength, but I guess not.'

'He didn't want you to go?'

'I couldn't stay.'

'No.' His fingers were under her hair, stroking at the nape of her neck, sending a little shiver down her spine.

'He just can't understand why I've done it though; he was happy. I suppose I was a bit bored or I would have asked him to come with me, wouldn't I? It just wasn't...'

'Enough?'

'No, it wasn't enough. It was just nice, but not very exciting, if you know what I mean?'

'I do.'

'I think he was ringing to check when I was going back.'

'Chloe never quite believed I wasn't going back. She went ballistic when the penny dropped.' His fingers paused for a moment then resumed their mesmerising game.

'But you didn't leave her because you were bored, did you? It wasn't like me and Si.'

'Probably nothing like you and Si, no.'

Kezia forgot they were sat in a field, forgot her arm was alternating between feeling on fire and prickling with pins and needles, and leaned in a bit closer, until she could smell his mix of soap and skin. 'You were in deep.'

'Too deep.' He rested his chin on the top of her head. 'We worked together, well, she was one of the managers and she was the hottest woman I'd ever met. She had a kind of sexual energy about her – power and looks. She wasn't what you'd call beautiful, but she was stunning.' He almost spat the word out, even though his voice was so low it was just for her. 'You couldn't ignore Chloe, and if she picked you out you weren't going to say no.'

James stared across the field, but he wasn't seeing the horses. He was seeing Chloe. Chloe in her power suit, killer heels and red lipstick.

It had been pure lust at first, but then he'd got to like her. And that was where it all started to go wrong. She'd sensed it, bided her time and gone in for the kill. At least that was how he saw it. She'd shown him up as her plaything and left him ashamed of where he'd let her lead him, and angry. Very angry.

'She was a few years older than me, pure fucking evil.'

'But she can't have been all bad?'

'Oh no, she could play the sweet and innocent, and then blow your mind with her sex games. Chloe was adventurous, what kind of a man doesn't want that?' What kind of a naïve idiot? 'It was all about her, she'd let you believe you had some control and then she'd gradually take over.' Until he was on his knees begging her, because that was how she liked it. At first he'd thought it was just fun, let her take the decisions, forced down his natural urges to be in charge, because he loved her, he wanted to please her. But then he discovered there was no way back. 'She'd got all kinds of tricks up her sleeve.'

'But you didn't have to stay, did you?' Her voice was just a soft trickle in the silence.

*You do when you're in too deep.* He'd been infatuated until it had turned to distrust, and then to hate. 'We'd made these videos. If it had come out at work it would have ruined me. And once she'd got me she knew how to turn me on. You can learn to like pain.' That emptiness he wanted to lose settled in his gut. She'd pushed him, twisted what they had. The nightmare a man thinks he wants, but finds out he doesn't.

*Let me tie you down, big boy. See how you like me being in charge.* She'd run one long scarlet nail down his chest, teased at his bottom lip with white teeth. She'd turned the tables. He loved pinning her down; having the normally powerful woman defenceless beneath him made him as hard as hell, made him want her more than ever. But her being on top did it for him too.

She'd cuffed him to the brass bedstead and then gone to get ready. And she'd come back in long black leather boots, elbow-length black gloves, black leather corset that held everything in but gave everything out. And it had started.

He'd never been as instantly rock hard as he had that time. He'd never felt the tease of a flogger, or the pain and when she finally let him come he'd never exploded and roared like he had that night.

And the game continued. She'd tease and torture him one day, beg him to spank her the next. She'd bring back girls, bring back toys. One day she was cougar, the next day cub. And each day he got pulled in deeper, craved more, until pushing the boundaries became an obsession he couldn't break

And the game continued.

Until he dared to stop it.

## Chapter 7

'I was infatuated, then one day she brought one of her exes along to play. He seemed a nice-enough guy. Until.' He stopped himself short. Too much talking. 'Some things are better left in the past.'

'You shouldn't put them there until you understand them.'

'I don't even understand you, Kezia.'

'Well you could always try harder. If, that is, you want to.'

'You know what? I do want to.'

Kez could listen to his voice all day, it was the purr of a cat, gentle, lulling, in tune with her senses so that it connected with something inside her every time.

The broad palm of his hand swept down her back sending her pulse rate up a notch, and when he got to his feet he took her with him. 'Come on, let's go and check you over properly. But first,' he smiled, 'I want you to do something.'

She was inches from him and he just had to know she was trembling, because no way was it just on the inside. She rested her hand against his chest to steady herself, and this time he didn't dodge away. Just covered it with his own, then gently lifted it away, but didn't drop it.

'Just go up to Red, slip the halter on and give him a pat and then take it off.' She raised an eyebrow. The man was on a different planet. 'Just so you know you can.' Which seemed a bit warped to her, just when he'd got her all psyched up and ready to go in an altogether better direction. She sighed, and his grin broadened into a smile. Which was sexy too. 'Do as you're told for once, woman.'

Red stood like a docile donkey, like he knew the rules and couldn't give a monkeys. Swine. She went back, handed the halter over and he put his arm around her and squeezed, which was a bit too brotherly for her liking, but what the heck.

'Ouch, watch the arm.'

He laughed again. And it was a little dose of heaven. 'Come on, let's go and examine it properly.'

'What's with his name then? Red?' They walked back towards the house, striding easily together, stepping in time, and it clicked in her head that the nervous anticipation which had been winding up inside her had dissipated like a cloud broken up by the breeze.

'Red, for red alert. He was always switched to red alert, from the day he was born. As soon as he found his feet he was ready to use them.'

'And you let me pick him, you bugger.' She mock-punched him.

'Your choice. Everything, as they say, is for a reason.'

He might have managed to disperse the tension while they were walking back, but as soon as she put a foot through the doorway it all came back.

Sex was easy when it was 'heat of the moment, can't possibly say no, just gotta do it' except he hadn't actually mentioned sex. But the way he was looking at her shouted it out like a klaxon. And he'd said he wanted to understand her, well, wasn't that Mr Sexpert's way?

'You look like Red in flight mode.'

*That about summed it up.* 'Gee ta, without the red hair I guess?'

'You guess.' His voice had dropped a tone or two and he lifted his hand, rested it under her hair, against the skin of her neck, in that familiar gesture of his which never failed to make her want to melt into his hands. 'Shall I have a proper look at your arm?'

*Yeah, and the rest.* A little shiver whispered its way down her back and all she could do was nod. If he looked at her arm he'd carry on touching her, and she'd use any excuse to keep those hands in contact with her skin.

'Please.' She'd try that again, with the volume switched up. Being left speechless was a new one on her. 'Yes, please.'

'Mind if we take your top off?'

Mind? Hell, her brain was screaming out 'strip!' Even if some tiny sensible part was whispering no.

She shook her head dumbly, tugging at her lower lip, flinching as she lifted her arms and a hint of pain stabbed at her. 'Here.' He helped strip the t-shirt off, dropping it on the floor. And then his hands were resting on the bare skin of her shoulders and it wasn't pain that was making her shiver.

'Okay?' The weight of his thumbs drifted up over her shoulder socket. She was getting used to that quirk of an eyebrow, that familiar half frown of concentration. She'd never get used to his touch, never be able to turn off the part of her brain that sent her body into overdrive. He massaged around the top of her arms, his touch deepening and the warm glow between her thighs intensified. 'It'll be fine. Sore, but fine.' The tips of his fingers skated over her breastbone, out over her breasts and her throat tightened. 'You'll be fine.' Fine, what kind of a word was fine? Meaningless. She didn't want to be fine, she wanted to feel on fire. She wanted to get lost in the moment, blast out the past. Forget everything except the right here and now.

Warm breath bathed her neck, firm lips slowly traced over the path his fingers had taken. 'Relax. Trust me.' She trusted. The relaxing bit was more difficult when every nerve ending in her body had switched to on. 'I do want to understand you, and I want to get to know every inch of you.' His voice was hoarse, rippling over her nerves, stirring her body up. 'But I don't want to hurt you, Kez. I'm not good for you.'

Yeah, well, hurt was the last thing she was thinking about now, in fact she couldn't think at all beyond the touch of his mouth on her skin.

'You won't hurt me.' *Just don't bloody stop now.*

'Kezia.' He did stop. Pulled away ever so slightly and fixed her with a look that made her want to jump on him and promise anything as long as he'd carry on doing what he was doing to her. 'I can't solve your problems. You want security.'

'I—'

'You said you were after permanence and I can't even promise tomorrow.'

'I don't want permanence from someone else.' She reached up, let her fingers thread through his hair. 'I can sort that bit on my own. I just want this, now.' She leaned in, her nostrils flaring to take in his scent. 'I've always lived in the moment, and I want this one.' Let her lips brush over his firm ones. 'Now.' And she wanted him. She just had to have him, even if it was the last thing she did.

His throat tightened, she watched the ripple of muscles down his throat as he swallowed. 'Be careful what you ask for.' His eyes narrowed, heavy with a hunger that looked like it matched her own, and she felt like she was on the edge of somewhere she hadn't been before. She'd been pushing him, baiting him, because she couldn't resist any longer. She needed another taste of what he'd given her before, but now she wanted more. The full works.

'I want you to kiss me, and,' she traced a finger down his throat, 'I want you to touch me and,' she swallowed, 'I want you to make me scream and moan.' She studied his collarbone like it was suddenly the most fascinating thing in the world. 'I want you to make me beg.' Oh, boy. Just saying it was making her damp.

He put a finger under her chin, tipped her head so that she was looking straight into his eyes. She'd never seen anyone look so serious, and look like they wanted her so much. 'Say that last bit again.'

'I want you to make me beg.'

His mouth covered hers and it wasn't a tender brush of lips, this was pure, barely restrained greed. And she was already on the verge of begging. How could the taste of his kiss make her thighs clench? He wrapped her hair around his hand, pulled her head back with a firmness that was on the edge of control, their teeth clashing as she grabbed out at his shirt. Needing something to hang on to, something to make her feel grounded.

She'd almost forgotten she was stripped to the waist, until his fingers slipped under the lace of her bra and firm fingers squeezed her nipple as he sucked on her tongue. Her pussy gave a tiny spasm. He pulled back slightly and she gasped.

'I'd quite like to fuck you on the kitchen table.' He grinned, and it was dangerous. 'But I know somewhere better.' He grabbed her hand, pulled her towards the stairs. 'Somewhere I can really make you beg.' Which sent another shiver straight to the throbbing area between her thighs. 'Anticipation,' he whispered against her neck, as he pushed open a door, and his breath shimmied down her body, leaving a trail of goose bumps, 'is everything.' His dry lips brushed against her skin and her heart pounded a bit harder.

'First, you're going to scream and then, you're going to beg.' His voice held the authority of a man who wanted much, much more, and suddenly she was afraid of how much he'd want her to give. This begging business had seemed fine when she thought she was leading the game, had found a way to drag something out of him, but she suddenly had a feeling she'd met her match.

'I don't think you need this.' He reached round and effortlessly unclasped her bra. Whatever happened to the fumbling and tugging that normally happened? The lace-covered cups tipped forward and she shivered as his gaze rested on her tightening nipples. He pulled her gently to her feet, expert hands undoing her belt. 'Or these.' She wriggled her hips, helping him pull the skin-tight jeans over her hips. He gave a low laugh that hit deep in her stomach. 'Like getting into Fort Knox.' Then he spotted the lacy knickers underneath. 'Though not much resistance once you get past the first barrier.' He tugged again, trying to peel the jeans further down, then suddenly gave her a shove that sent her sprawling back on the bed.

'Hey.'

'Hey nothing. I'm not being beaten by a pair of jeans.' Then he grabbed hard and peeled them down so that they turned inside out, holding them up triumphantly. 'Next time it'll be the scissors.' She was laughing, but the way he said it hitched up the anticipation inside her. He meant it.

He held a hand out, eased her back to her feet and she instinctively reached a hand up to cover her breasts.

'Don't.' He was looking her over in a way she'd never been looked at before. Who stopped to look when they'd got to the practically naked bit? But it was bloody hard to just stand there uncovered, bloody hard not to fidget. 'Don't you want me to see?'

And she did, she wanted him to look at her, she wanted it to turn him on. She let her hands skate down her body, slide down to hang by her sides. Let him look.

'You're beautiful.' His lips brushed over hers, his hands rested on her waist, moved up together until they cupped her breasts, his thumbs against her nipples with a touch that was barely there.

The shiver that prickled its way over her skin went deeper, set each part of her body on edge. Waiting. She let out the breath she'd been holding, tried not to sway her body in time with the mesmerising stroke of his thumbs.

'I want to do things to you that nobody else ever has. I want,' his fingers stilled and she stopped breathing, 'you to let me do whatever I want.'

Her stomach muscles tightened. He was saying just the right things to make every bit of her want to cry out to him, and he was saying it like he meant it.

'Will you let me?'

She dampened suddenly dry lips with her tongue. She's almost forgotten the getting to know each other better bit. She just wanted him. Wanted him to do whatever he wanted because whatever he said, he already knew her. Knew what she wanted deep down. What she needed. And she wanted him to give up a bit of himself, to remember how to share. She was just scared that in the process she'd give too much, lose something she didn't want to. And he'd run scared and take a part of him with her.

He was waiting. He was as still as it was possible to be. And it didn't matter what she risked losing. Her heart ached for him, for the man she knew he was deep down, but her body throbbed with need, and right now he was the only person who could meet it. She nodded, the slightest movement as she stared into his eyes, eyes that were almost black and for a second he looked like he was scared too.

Then he leant forward and kissed her, a brief dry brushing of lips that was far more tempting than any lingering, damp kiss of the past had ever been. 'Close your eyes, Kezia.' She closed them, felt the brush of silk against her cheek before he tightened the band of material around her head.

Oh God, she was wet. She tried to stop the moan threatening to burst from her lips. She was aware of the dampness that had built up trickling down between her thighs.

'Turn around.'

She turned, wobbling, disorientated. Lost without sight, or his touch.

'Put your hands behind your back.' She did, heard the wood on wood of a drawer opening, felt the rough rub of rope against her wrists as he bound them. Heard the pounding of blood in her ears as her pulse raced faster. The front of her thighs were pressed against the bed, and it dipped slightly as he sat and moved things, pushing what had to be pillows against her.

The warmth of his hand was between her shoulder blades, his other on the front of her shoulder. 'Lean forward on to the pillows.' He'd piled up the cushions so that her legs were still straight when she tipped forward to lie, and now she could barely move. Off balance with her hands tied behind her there was no way she could get up without rolling to the side. And for some strange reason it didn't panic her. He brushed her hair from her face and stood, the bed lifting slightly as he went. 'Now open your legs.'

Oh, God, this was turning her on. This wasn't real. Except she could feel the dampness of her knickers, feel her juices building as her body rested against the softness of the satin cushions. She'd had dreams like this, dreams where she couldn't do anything to stop the man she lusted after.

He ran the tip of his finger between her buttocks and she clenched instinctively, and couldn't stop the little whimper. One hand held her cheeks apart and his finger circled her arsehole, sending a ripple of anticipation straight to her clit. 'Can I do whatever I want, Kez?' She hadn't realised how close he was to her. She'd been concentrating on what he was about to do and his soft voice near her ear made her whole body clench. He chuckled, slid his finger along her slit. 'Can I?'

'Yeeesss.' She could hardly breathe, let alone talk, so it came out as a strangled whisper.

'You are so gorgeous.' His finger moved gently along her swollen folds again, pressed slightly more firmly, slid just inside and a moan slipped from her. His other hand stroked softly down her inner thigh, a thigh that trembled as the tips of his fingers teased her. And then his cool breath whispered down her cunt and she gasped at the new sensation, just as he slipped his finger deep inside, so deep that she squirmed, rocking her hips to get more of him. 'Greedy girl.' He pulled the finger out, pushed two inside, just deep enough to rest against her g-spot, to bring the sudden sharper pang of need. And she realised she was panting. His fingers thrust gently in and out, a steady rhythm, a pressure that was building up inside her. She opened her legs wider, willing the pleasure to heighten, lifting her body as much as she could so that her legs shook as she balanced on tiptoe. Then the cold hit her. The ice-cold pressure against her burning clit, a vibrating coolness that made her cry out as she came in a violent, unexpected explosion. Not a gently built up orgasm, but a shattering she had no control of. He rocked the vibrator against her swollen nub, pressing his fingers firm against her slick channel and her body was trapped, pulsing, aching until she was shuddering, afraid she'd never stop.

Her body slowed, but he didn't stop. 'Please.' God, he had to stop, she'd combust.

He laughed. 'This is where it gets better. Trust me.' Her thighs quivered as he ran one finger, damp with her juices, slowly up the length of her leg, until it rested against the heat of her labia. Slowly he parted the lips. The cradling warmth of his breath was a warning, and then the fluid in his mouth mixed with the dampness from her body. He licked along her, his tongue prodding and probing until she ached with need. And then he sucked, teased at her lips, tugged at her throbbing clit. It was torture; the thin line between heaven and hell. The desire to stop him; the need to beg him to carry on.

He thrust his tongue deeper, lapped at her juices. She opened her legs wider, shivered with the need to have him inside, let him in until she couldn't open any wider, until the ripples started to build and as his tongue swirled new sensations inside her, she came again.

The cool metal of his belt was against her hip, brushed over her bottom and then she felt his dampness. Smelled his pre-come as he rubbed over her, nudged at her entrance. He undid the ties on her wrists as his hard, rough thighs pressed against her own soft skin. He unwrapped her eyes and moved her arms up until they were above her head, held only by his large hand and as he gazed into her eyes he thrust hard, once. Burying himself deeply inside her, all the way. Slowly he drew out and thrust hard back in. Then he pulled out.

She licked her tongue over dry lips. 'Please.'

He pushed so hard back in that the moan was mixed with a scream.

'Fuck me, hard.'

His hands shifted to her hips, his fingers curled into her, held her tight as he pulled her back towards him, thrust harder. She felt him grow, felt him get warmer, felt his cock start to throb inside her as he moved faster. And she was coming, her pussy grasping greedily at him as he grunted and gave one last hard thrust, his grip on her tightening as he shut his eyes.

He eased her back onto the bed and lay beside her, and she wrapped her leg over his, her fingers playing with the hairs on his chest. And as she stroked him, his cock started to stir again. His fingers tightened in her hair.

'Behave, woman.'

'How do you know I'm not? Your eyes are shut.'

'I can tell.' He shifted his body so that his own was across hers, pinning her down. Kezia wriggled and tried to object, but her body felt heavy. Now she knew what 'sated' meant. She closed her eyes, just for a moment.

He was dreaming, but he wasn't, which meant he should open his eyes. But he didn't want to because that could spoil everything. He fought to keep his breathing even, to not let her know he was awake, but it was a battle he couldn't win. He reached out, threaded his fingers through the silky hair, holding her head lightly – not wanting to force his cock deeper into her throat, but not wanting her to stop.

She gave a small chuckle, the tremor catching in her throat, which clutched at the tip of his engorged dick. And he groaned, groaned louder as her fingers closed around his throbbing balls, massaging, stroking. Shit, that was good.

Slowly, painstakingly slowly, so that his fingers curled against her scalp with need, her tongue licked a path from his balls to the tip of his hardening cock. She circled the tip, flicking her tongue, squeezing him gently with hands that were plying him with just the right amount of pressure. He gritted his teeth, stared at the ceiling and tried not to explode in her mouth. The warmth of her mouth slid along the length of him, the pressure of her lips just firm enough to tease him, to hold him. He gasped as she slowly sucked her way back up, the tips of her teeth catching his skin with the lightest of touches. Then she paused, looked at him, her hazel eyes tinged with a mossy colour. Her hand slid up and down, smoothly gliding over the slick skin, her thumb rolling over his tip each time she reached the top.

He'd not woken up with a woman in his bed for years. He'd not had a woman sleep in his bed for years. He went to theirs, and then he left before the mark was overstepped, before the questions, demands and needs could be voiced.

She was still watching him, still rubbing him with a pressure and warmth he didn't want to stop.

'Tell me.' She didn't take her gaze off him, but her tongue swept over him, the tip leaving a damp warmth in its wake, circling gently over his tip, around the rim, spreading the pearled drops of pre-come until the purplish bloom glistened and his stomach clenched with need.

'Don't stop.' His words were guttural in his ears. 'Suck me, Kez.' She closed her eyes as though to taste him better, dipped her head, sucked him in until his tip was against the back of her throat, until he almost came. His fingers tightened in her hair, not to hold her there but to stop himself thrusting. 'Make me come, Kezia.' Her tongue was fluttering against him, caressing the sensitive V at his tip, and all he could feel was the heat building, the need and then her mouth slipped from him. She ran her tongue over her lips.

'I want you inside me.' Her voice had a rough edge, and it was all the warning he had before she was astride him, her slick pussy poised above him. She lowered until he was nudging at her entrance, lowered until he could feel her heat, her juices. His hands tightened around her hips as she lowered herself, and he watched his cock disappear inside her. Slowly she started to move and he couldn't drag his gaze away from the point where their bodies joined, watched each time as he disappeared inside her. Her breath was speeding up, she was panting, her thighs trembling as she threw her head back and as he gripped her hips tighter he pushed back, forced himself deeper, thrust in time with her rise and fall. She started to come just before he did, the tiny trembles inside, the grasping walls of her closing around him and he couldn't control it any longer. As she slowed, he pushed harder, plunged one last time as hard as he could until release came. She felt him come, tightened around him and then slowly dropped on to his chest. And for the first time in years he wrapped his arms around someone, felt her heart hammering against his until they'd both slowed.

She groaned. 'I think I need a shower.' But she didn't move. 'I know I do.' With another groan she rolled off him, covering her eyes with her arm. 'I think that bloody horse came in and trampled me in my sleep.'

He laughed. And the sight of her rolling in his sheets, with her hair mussed up and her slender limbs in all directions tugged at something in his chest. It made him wonder if he should be here at all. She was cute and she was wholesome, well wholesome in a horny way. In a way he wanted to prove to himself that he could let go a little, could get closer to someone without feeling trapped. And yesterday Kezia seemed the perfect person to do that with. But even with her free-and-easy attitude, even with her giving as freely as most people took, he recognised she had a need. He wasn't so cut off that he couldn't see when someone had a gaping hole in their life. Using Kez to make himself feel more normal would be the cruellest thing he could do, would make him the bastard he'd sworn he'd never be – the spectre he'd run from just before it got too late.

'You're staring at me.'

'I'm not.' He put his hands behind his head. Out of temptation's way. Maybe now they'd both surrendered they wouldn't crave each other in the same way. Maybe now all he had to do was slowly step back, and she'd let him.

'You're not a bad shag, you know.' She rolled back over to look at him, hair across her face. He resisted the urge to brush it back.

'You give good head.' He grinned to show it was light-hearted.

'Thank you kind sir. I really wish I could be arsed to get up.'

'This might help.' He pushed her butt with his foot, slowly edged her towards the side of the bed. She didn't resist, just went, rolled out and onto her knees. Then turned and put her chin on the side of the bed.

'Bossy man.'

'I am.'

He watched. Nothing submissive about her this morning. No, he'd been the one admitting his need. Except with Kez it was about surrender, not submission like it had been with Chloe. With Chloe it was about giving in, in the hope of getting something back, of force and power. With Kez it was all letting go, admitting what you wanted. And as she'd done it for him, he'd wanted to do it back. Which scared the hell out of him.

Fuck, why was he letting Chloe into his head, even now? He closed his eyes.

'You don't need to worry you know, I can't get involved any more than you can.' Her voice was as soft as he'd heard it, but he daren't look at her. He kept his eyes shut. 'I want to settle down someday, I want to start now, but I can't.' She seemed to take a deep breath. 'I want to be here next week, next year but I don't know where I'll be. I don't know who killed my Mum and Dad, but I know why. And that scares me.'

He heard her resigned sigh as she stood up. She didn't shower in his room, just went out on quiet feet and he heard her own door open, then shut behind her.

Fuck, fuck, fuck. Which was worse? Thinking about everything that was wrong, or worrying about everything that was right? He wanted to ask what she meant, but asking meant knowing more, getting involved. He cursed again under his breath, swung his legs out of bed and headed for a cold shower.

'You like horses more than people don't you?' Kezia dumped another load of horseshit in the barrow. She was getting good at this. It was so easy, even a moron like her could get it right

'They don't ask questions all the time.' His tone was dry, but easy. 'Horses always do one of two things, fight or flight. And they'll always opt for the second if they have a choice.'

'They're quite proud though, aren't they? I mean they kind of do what they want?' She'd watched them from her bedroom window in the evenings, milling around, bossing each other. If James went out they followed him; it was like he was an honorary horse, and she didn't get it. He didn't feed them, no titbits, no bribes, and he didn't boss them around. No surrendering going on there. Except he *was* in control, they wanted him to like them. Just like she did. She stabbed at the straw bed angrily. He was turning her into a bloody horse.

He raised an eyebrow.

'What?'

'Don't "what" at me like that.' His voice was mild.

'Why do they like you and not me?'

'It's by invitation.' He smiled. 'You need to ask nicely.' The wicked light was in his eye. 'Like you did last night.'

'Huh.'

'Come on.' He held out his hand.

'What's that for?' She looked at him suspiciously. He'd been edgy at breakfast, then slowly unwound. But it narked her. He'd been thinking about that woman, making comparisons. She just knew it. And this spoiled everything, even if everything was supposed to be nothing.

'The teacher,' he cocked an eyebrow mischievously, 'is going to teach.' He led her to the tack room and passed her a halter. 'Go grab Sparky.'

'Why Sparky? Why not Red?'

'Sparks will teach you—'

'I thought you were the teacher?'

95

'Sparks will teach you better than I can, Red does advanced lessons.' He was still grinning, as though she amused him. Oh well, at least she was good for entertainment value. 'You can learn a lot from a horse if you're prepared to listen.'

She raised an eyebrow, shrugged, unsure sure if she cared right now. She was miffed. He'd made her miffed, and she was trying not to be, which made it worse. And now he was pretending to be nice. Maybe if he'd kicked her out of bed properly it would have been better; if he'd done his moody bit and stomped off down to the river. But he hadn't.

'You too tired for lessons? Did I wear you out?' He looked all innocence, but he was trying to wind her up. She stuck her tongue out and went to get the horse. He was on a starvation paddock and so easy to catch, even for a moron like her. But he was not too impressed when he was led, or rather dragged, straight into the indoor school.

'Sit there and watch. You're good at watching.' He'd got his bossy voice on again, which reminded her of last night. So she gritted her teeth and tried to do much the same thing with her thighs, and won a grin. 'You'll be good at this bit, making him run away.'

'Smart arse.'

He laughed easily and marched towards Sparky, who lifted his head and walked off a few steps. Just a few; he wasn't prone to using up energy unnecessarily.

'You're just herding him.' This looked boring.

'Kind of, I'm sending him away, not letting him be with me.' He stopped. The horse stopped. He sent him on again. 'Now we're going to turn him and go the other way.' He stopped after a few circuits, and Sparky stopped, turned in, watching. He sent him off again.

'This is getting boring, if you don't mind me saying. What's the point?'

James gave a low chuckle. 'Watch his ears, watch his head and his mouth. At some point he'll want to start being with me, his

96

ears will be on me, he'll lower his head, mouth.'

'Like a baby.'

'Yup.' He turned the horse, sent him off again, and for the first time she noticed his ears. Tuned in, flickering in James' direction. 'He'll stop wanting to run and he'll start asking if he can be friends soon.'

'Begging, you mean.' She sounded dry, she knew it.

'Hey, don't knock it.' He was laughing at her, or with her. She still wasn't quite sure. 'And when he's really keen I'll invite him in.' The horse was still, head lowered, chewing, waiting. James walked past with that easy, quiet gait and the horse followed, shadowed him around the arena, and mimicked him each time he paused or changed direction, until they ended up by Kez. He ran a hand down the horse's neck, then he kissed her. Her, not the horse. A soft fleeting brush of lips that she could have imagined.

'Now you do it.'

A quiet challenge.

So she did. At first it wasn't as easy as it looked, nothing ever was. She moved too quickly and he threw his head up, went off at a spanking pace, which was a bloody miracle for Sparks. And when she tried to turn him he spun, carried on the same way. But then she got it. She toned it down and did less, listening to the horse. She got it. He wanted to be with her; he chose to follow her. He trusted her to do the right thing.

He followed her back to James, who had a soft smile on his face that made him almost look gentle. She brushed her lips over his, mimicking what he'd done to her and handed over the halter. He felt her heart tighten inside her chest like someone had hold of it.

He took it, his gaze never wavering. 'What did you mean about your parents?'

'Eh?' She knew what he was getting at, but wasn't sure if she should tell him. Even if she did trust him with her thoughts, worse still, her body. But hopes and fears, who did you share those with?

Her mobile buzzed in her pocket for the umpteenth time that

day. There was only one person it could be. Simon. She ignored it.

'Why Kez? Why were they killed?' And for the first time since she'd spotted him, when she'd been swaying on the top of that five-barred gate like a crazy woman, she was scared.

# Chapter 8

'I'm not sure…'

'What? If you tell me you might have to kill me?' She guessed he was joking to cover up the awkward moment. The moment they both realised that he actually wanted to know.

'Something like that.' She looked down at the arena floor, scuffed a track in the surface with her toes. Maybe she was being dramatic, stupid. But it had been easier to keep things inside, to run away, all the time telling herself she was doing it because she needed to. She needed security, to build a life. Yeah, that was a big part of it, but so was the fact that she was scared. Scared that it might not all be over.

'You're buzzing.'

And there was that, too, bloody Simon, who seemed determined not to let her go. He'd always struck her as an easygoing, casual type. She hadn't thought for a single second that he might be taking it, them, seriously. There hadn't been a 'them'. No one had ever mentioned sticking together; she just thought they'd been passing time before life moved on. She had a host of fond memories, and she'd thought he was happy to join the others. 'I know I am. It's Simon, and he's not giving me good vibrations right now.'

James smiled. 'You want to answer it?'

'Nope.'

'Might get him off your back.'

'Might make it worse.' She wasn't exactly trying to dodge him, it just seemed sense not to give him attention. Not to let him think she cared.

'Come on let's get Sparky back in his field.'

She turned, and the big horse was practically peering down her neck. But he didn't seem quite so big any more. 'It's all about advance and retreat isn't it? Knowing when to push and when to back off.'

'You already knew that, though.'

'Maybe I'm too pushy sometimes.'

'Maybe you want things too much sometimes.'

'They know when you mean it, though, don't they.' She ran her hand down the sleek neck and scratched at his withers. 'And they know how to give up control without—' she paused, abandoning their self-respect? Giving in altogether?

'They let you take charge because they want you to, putting faith in you.' He held out his hand, inches above hers and waited. And she took it because she wanted to. And she sometimes bloody wished she had someone who could take charge.

James moved to put the horse's halter on.

'Won't he just follow us without a halter?' He'd just followed them around like he wanted to be there. That was the deal wasn't it?

He gave a small, low laugh that tickled the hairs on the back of her neck. 'Sparks is his own man, open this gate and he'll be off. A bit like you, he takes liberties.'

They walked easily side by side, let Sparky back into his field, watched him amble over to the far fence and gaze longingly at the lush grass on the other side. Always greener, wasn't it?

'Can we go down to the river?'

He nodded, didn't question.

She listened to the water murmuring past, the odd nicker in the distance from a contented horse, watched the shadows shimmer around them as the slight breeze let the leaves lift and fall.

'It was because of the drugs.' She slowly pulled the petals off the flower she had picked, turning it, picking them off one at a time. 'They were killed because Dad was stupid enough to think he could sort things on his own.' She pulled her knees up to her chest and rested her chin on them. She stared at the water and tried to ignore the image of her parents, hand in hand, laughing. She plucked another flower from near her feet. 'If they hadn't had a blow-out he would have never known, he wouldn't have found them and that would have been it.'

It had been a hot day, they'd been buried deep in the countryside driving along roads for miles without seeing another person. She didn't often travel with them these days, she went her own way, often hitching, but they always reached the same destination and met up in a lot of their old haunts. She'd have a stretch on her own, sometimes weeks, months and then bump into them at the places that they all loved best along the route.

But this summer had been different. They'd been thinking of packing it in, settling somewhere. This summer had been the last one they'd probably do this and so she'd made sure that she was in the same places at the same times. They'd been travelling in tandem, she was riding pillion with Simon on his motorbike. He'd offered her a ride a few weeks earlier and they'd hit it off and stuck together. He was easy company, good for a laugh and happy to go wherever the mood took him, which just then was with Kezia.

He hadn't been like them, permanently on the road. He was a steady income, one house, one mortgage, job in the suburbs kind of guy. But he said he'd promised himself one year of easy living, one last year of fun before it was too late, then back to the grindstone. And it had been nice to have a friend along, nice to hold onto his body as they travelled through the countryside, nice to hold onto him at night.

So when her dad had lifted the boot to dig out the spare tyre, she'd been there, and so had Simon. By his side, helping like she had since she'd been a kid.

'They had this old car, so it had a spare.' She glanced briefly over at him and he didn't even nod. Nothing about him moved. 'And when he pulled it out, it was packed. He knew what it was, I mean we'd come across enough people who did drugs of some kind or another. I mean, they weren't druggies but they smoked; I guess they were just that sixties era who'd never stopped.' All flower power, live and let live. Her parents hadn't really been part of that scene, they'd just one day decided they wanted a different kind of life so they'd sold everything but the car, given up their responsibilities and moved on to what they'd thought would be better. They wanted to explore, to live, to discover the world, they said.

'Was it someone you knew then that planted the stuff?'

'I don't think so. You see, although we travelled around we had a kind of set route. We didn't stop in any particular place, but I suppose we followed the work. We'd be in the right place when it came to grape-picking time, or oranges, then somewhere else when there were music festivals, you know. There's always a best time to be everywhere so I suppose people could work out where we'd be heading to next. I think someone knew where we were going and decided we'd do a good job of carrying the stuff for them.'

'Or just second-guessed where you were off to.'

She looked up and those midnight eyes were clear. Fathom-deep, un-muddied pools.

'It would be easy to put the stuff in the car, it didn't even lock properly.' It had never needed to be locked, no one would have nicked it. 'Dad went to the police, they talked to all of us, the other guys working on the same job, all that kind of thing.' She hugged her knees closer in. 'We thought that was it, and then he got this note.'

Notes like that belonged in books, in the movies, not real life. It wasn't even a veiled threat. It was a threat. Black and white. A threat of what would happen if he answered any more questions, if he went back to the police. If he changed his plans.

'He took it to the police.' She glanced over at James again and knew that she didn't need to say anything else. Not that she wanted to think about the scruffy station and the officer who didn't seem to care. He'd not even kept it for evidence.

'They haven't caught them, have they?'

She shook her head. 'I keep thinking they're going to come after me.'

'It's over, why would they want you?'

'I don't know.' She shrugged. 'It's just a feeling.' A feeling that it hadn't finished, that there were loose ends. Her. A feeling that spread into her dreams with flames that licked around her, hotter and hotter. And a feeling that Simon, was right if they wanted her they'd find her.

'Who knows you're here?'

'Marie.' She gave a little shrug of her shoulders.

'Only Marie?'

'There isn't anyone else. Apart from the police, of course. I had to talk to them when I got off the plane to tell them how to get hold of me.'

He'd moved closer without her knowing, and somehow his arm was around her shoulders. 'You'll be fine.'

'I know. I don't want to leave here, though, not yet.'

'You won't have to.' He rested his chin on her head. He was making promises he couldn't keep. 'Does Marie know any of this?'

'Nobody does.' She leaned in a bit closer, into his warmth. 'Can we forget it now?'

'Or you'll have to kill me?'

'Yeah.' She wasn't managing to forget it. 'I mean, if they'd been interested in me I would have found out before I left for Italy wouldn't I?' It was the question she'd asked herself a million times, when she'd woken up from nightmares that crackled with fire and blood and she was sweating and shaking. It was over for them, whoever they were. She'd packed her rucksack, grabbed her guitar and ran. She'd had to put as many miles between that burning car and herself as she could to try and outrun the nightmares and pretend it never happened. A friend had told her about the centre in Capri and she'd grabbed at the chance of going there. Gentle, calming luxury while she got her head together and made a plan. Whoever had killed her parents had made their point and moved on. And now she had to. And that had been the plan, to rebuild her life somewhere new, a totally different life. But sometimes forgetting was harder than it looked.

'I guess so.' He tipped back abruptly, taking her with him so that he was lying flat out and she pressed against him, her head on his chest, and the sound of his heart hammering in her ear took over from the babble of water.

When they'd been in bed he'd had his arm around her in that lazy, knackered-from-a-good-shag kind of way, but this time he felt different. He was holding her like he wanted to do.

'Don't worry, we'll sort it.'

'You think your Roisin will give me a job, then?' She traced her finger over his chest, let the tip thread its way into his shirt so she could feel the heat of his skin.

'She's not my Roisin.'

The button popped so that her whole hand could slip in.

'But I reckon you're getting good at making them belt round the arena. I can pass the message on if you like?' His voice was serious so she dared look up under her eyelashes at him. His eyes were closed. She rested her head back down, let her hand explore a bit more, watching as the bulge at his crotch became more defined.

He might sort 'it', but she seriously wanted to sort him. It was becoming an addiction, he touched her and she had to touch right back.

'You better stop that.' His voice was a lazy drawl, tinged with that husky edge that made her want to carry on.

'You really want me to stop?' She brushed her lips against his throat and his muskiness turned her on a bit more. She was going to bury her nose in a minute if she didn't watch herself. Not a good move.

'Just because,' in an instant he'd rolled, trapped her body under his, 'I let you take me earlier, doesn't mean,' he'd caught her wrists, pinned them above her head, 'you're the one in control.'

Kez tried to ignore the sudden buzz that headed straight to her clit. 'You reckon?'

'I know.' Her voice might have had a hoarse edge to it; his was pure sex. 'And you'd do well to remember.' His mouth came down on her neck, his teeth teasing at the skin and then he sucked, hard. Her pussy clenched and she knew she was already damp. Expectant.

'Much as I'd like to shag you senseless, I'm not going to.' Those dark eyes were staring intently into hers from only inches away. She shifted her hips, rubbed against the hard bulge of his erection. His eyes narrowed and he chuckled. A firm hand came down between her legs, hard fingers pressing against her. 'The next time I do you're going to beg.' He pressed a bit harder, watching her. 'I love watching you when you're turned on, when you're just about to come.' The pressure lifted and he stroked along her with a light touch that scorched straight through the fabric and made her squirm even more. Rubbed up and down until she lifted her pelvis, tipping herself against him. 'Later, Kez.' His mouth came down over hers and she opened instinctively. Let his taste mingle with hers. He pulled away, her wrists still pinned down by his hand, his knee across her legs.

She nibbled at her lower lip. 'You're a tease.'

'Me?' The low chuckle made it worse. 'I'd love to do more than tease, but I've got to get up to the house.'

It felt like she was pouting, and from his laugh she probably was. 'Why? I'm feeling horny now.'

He groaned. Dipping his head, he kissed the part of her stomach that had bared when he'd raised her arms. 'You don't really do demure do you?'

'You don't really want demure, do you?'

One shake of his head, then he let go and jumped to his feet. 'There's someone in the yard, or I'd be showing you exactly what I want.'

'How do you know?' She stayed where she was, flopped out on the ground. Not quite willing to give up yet.

'Sorry.' He held out his hand to help her up. 'I really,' yanked her closer so that he could kiss her, and she could feel him against her thigh, 'am.' His mouth was hard against hers for a moment as he held her head in both hands and came down with a pressure that made her reel and her lips almost smart. Then he took a step back, half turned. 'Come on. Quick before I tear those knickers off.'

'Really?' Well, if there was still a chance....

'Stop it.' He waved a finger. 'Someone could be stealing all the horses while I'm tying you to a tree.'

'Tying? Oo.' Sounded good to her.

He took a step up the bank. Raised one eyebrow in a way that put her on edge, if she could become any edgier. 'I could always tie you up, so I know where you'll be when I get back.'

She took a step away. He looked serious.

'In fact, that idea is really starting to appeal to me. I could tie you,' he pushed his hands into his pockets, which somehow made him look even more dangerous, 'I wouldn't even need to gag you, no one around here to hear your screams.' Her heart sped up a notch. 'Then I can come back and—'

He took one step back towards her and Kezia dodged around him, scrambling up the bank on shaking legs. Because even though that felt like the biggest turn on yet, she wasn't sure if the reality scared her or thrilled her.

He caught up with her easily, his long, effortless stride eating up the ground, slipping his hand into hers in a way that she could never have said no to.

'How do you know there's someone in the yard?'

'There's a buzzer.' He grinned. 'Didn't you hear it?'

'My ears aren't as big as yours.' He was more switched on than the horses; talk about red alert. 'But there isn't a buzzer, I couldn't find one when I got here.'

'There is, Miss Know-it-all. It's a sensor. Walk through the gateway and it triggers. We don't need a push bell, we know if there's someone about.'

'So you knew I was on the gate?'

'I could sense danger.' He raised an elegant eyebrow and the grin widened, making her stomach give a little hiccup.

She thumped him with her free hand. 'Even you can't do that.'

'Well, actually I'd come out to check the horses and saw you.'

'So, who is it?'

'Even I don't know that.'

'Smart arse.'

'We're not expecting any deliveries, so I don't know who the hell it is. We don't exactly get a lot of visitors, so if he's selling something he's just about to find out I'm not buying.'

James dropped her hand to open the gate, pulled it shut behind them and when she turned she immediately spotted the figure heading their way.

He was blond, tanned and had a smile on his face as he waved casually in their direction.

'Bugger.' She muttered it under her breath, but James obviously heard it. He seemed to move closer to her. 'That would be Simon.'

'And what the hell is Simon doing here?' There was a tightness back in his voice, the one that had been there when she'd arrived, when he hadn't wanted her to stay. 'Did you know he was coming?'

'Well, I didn't exactly know. He left a message when I didn't answer his calls. Said we needed to chat properly, but I didn't think he'd turn up.' Why hadn't he listened? Why hadn't he just let it all end like it was supposed to? 'He's supposed to be in Italy.'

'So, you're going to chat?' There was an edge of sarcasm to his voice.

'Guess so. What else am I supposed to do?'

'Show him the door?'

'Don't be daft.' She glanced up at him for the first time since she'd spotted Simon; he looking like he was being serious. 'I can't just refuse to talk to him.' He was standing by the edge of the stable block, hands in pockets as though unsure whether to head their way or not. Kezia took a deep breath and started to walk towards him.

'Hey, surprise.' He grinned, looked from her to James. 'Pleased to see me?' Leaning in to kiss her, he left his hand on her shoulder as though he owned her. She resisted the urge to shake him off.

'Why've you come here, Simon?' It made her feel sad, mean. 'I did tell you…'

'I wanted to see you.' He ruffled her hair, gave her his hangdog look. 'I thought you'd be pleased. And,' he smiled, a smile that didn't quite reach his eyes, 'I thought you'd be bored with all this and ready to hit the road again.'

'I don't want to hit the road, Simon.'

'Come on, let's chat.' He took a hold of her hand, a gentle tug, which meant he wanted to lead her away from James.

'No.' She pulled back, shoved her hands deep in her pockets. 'There isn't anything to talk about. I'm happy here.'

'With him?' There was a slightly scornful edge and he was looking at James, then back at her.

'This isn't about James, Simon. It's about me.'

'Don't be silly, Kez. This isn't you, being stuck in some hole in the middle of nowhere forever.'

'I didn't say it's forever, and it isn't a hole.'

'You need to be free. Come on, Kez.' His voice had softened, wheedling. 'What would your parents think? This isn't what they wanted.'

'How do you know what they wanted? You hardly knew them, you hardly know me.'

'I know you well enough. After all we did.'

'We didn't "do" anything.'

'We did enough for me to know what's good for you. And I know your Mum and Dad wouldn't have wanted to see you stuck here in the type of place they escaped from.'

'No, you don't know. They were going to pack the big adventure in, did you know that? No, you didn't, did you? This was the last summer on the road, then they were coming back here.'

'But you weren't going to come with them. You hate being stuck, Kez.'

'I want to be stuck.' *But I didn't grow up and realise until they'd gone.*

'Don't be silly, this place will drive you nuts. And so will sticking at one job, what are you going to do,' he glanced around, 'muck out the same bloody stables for the rest of your life? You can't cut that kind of life.'

'You're wrong, Simon.'

'Okay,' his voice had softened down again, 'I know you're all cut up still, I get that you're upset, but you're not being sensible. Come back with me, we'll take it slow until you get back to normal.'

'I am fucking normal, don't you get that Simon?'

'It's him, isn't it? He's talked you into this, made you think you can live his kind of boring life.'

'I thought you were the one with the boring life, it was you who was having a fun year out.'

'You made me realise what I was missing. I want to be with you, Kez, we're made for each other. I'm not stupid enough to jack it in and go back to being a suit.'

'Well, I've never been one, and call me stupid but I am ready to jack it all in.'

'You'll regret it.'

'My choice.' *Why didn't he just give in and go?*

'You heard her.' It was the first thing James had said. She'd almost forgotten he was there, brooding behind her.

'You have got to come with me, Kez.'

'She hasn't got to do anything.'

109

'Why can't you keep out of this, mate? You don't understand.'

'Simon.' She spoke softly, wanting to drop the confrontation, wanting to make him understand, make him go away. 'I'm sorry, but I'm not coming.'

He stared at her, and it was a blank, unpleasant look she hadn't seen on his face before. 'You'll regret this. I can look after you, he can't.' He took a step back. 'No one else can. I'll come back tomorrow afternoon and pick you up. You need me, Kez, whether you like it or not.'

'Simon.' But he ignored it and marched back across the yard. Then the roar of his motorbike filled her head as he kicked it into action. She stared through the gate as he drove away, doubt creeping into her thoughts. He was right, he could look after her. He knew her, knew what she'd been through, maybe he knew her better than she did herself. Maybe she was a fool for thinking she could start again and thinking she could change everything. She'd been happy once, in her old life, with her parents. She'd been content to accept things as they were. Who was she to think it had all been wrong, that there was something better?

'Maybe he's right. Maybe I don't belong here. I can't do anything useful anyway.'

'Bollocks. You aren't rejecting what your parents wanted, you did that bit and now you've got to do what's right for you.'

'And what's that?' She scuffed at the dirt with her toes, not wanting to look at him.

'Only you know the answer to that one, Kezia. But, you can do whatever you want. He's the stupid one, not you for trying.'

'Is it worth even trying?'

She glanced up then and he was staring at her, straight into her soul. 'You don't need me to answer that.' And he walked off.

Two men walking out on her in two minutes flat. Must be a record. She stared out at the horses, not really seeing them. She'd thought she knew what she wanted. But did she? And what did Simon mean when he said only he could look after?

## Chapter 9

'I thought nobody knew where you were?' He was angry, angry at the twat who had just turned up, angry at the way he'd been so familiar, angry that one word from him and she was thinking of jacking it all in. Going back to her old life and giving up what she'd achieved here.

'Maybe I told him.' She shrugged and sat down at the pine table. 'He went with me to Italy, so he met Marie, maybe she told him. I don't know, but what does it matter anyway?'

'Don't listen to what he said, Kez, your parents would be proud of you.'

'Says the man who's not seen his for years.'

'You don't know anything about that.'

'Well, bloody tell me, then.'

'You can't just give up.'

'See? You've just avoided saying a word, like you always do.'

'And you're avoiding answering me.' He put his cup down carefully, before he gave in to the urge to throw it. 'Why did he come here? Did you ask him to?'

'No, I fucking didn't, and if you don't stop interrogating me I'm walking, right now. Okay?'

'I just don't want to see you making a mistake.' *Going off with a dork. Going, full stop.* Losing his temper wasn't going to help, but nobody seemed to be able to get to him quite like she did, nobody since Chloe. But he didn't want to think of them in the same sentence. 'Look.' He sat down. He just needed to control this conversation, stop it spiralling into something it shouldn't. 'I thought you liked it here?' *I thought you liked me.*

'I do.' She traced a finger over the whorls in the wood. 'But maybe it isn't what they would have wanted.'

'I think your parents would have wanted you to be true to yourself. That's what they tried to do, isn't it? To be the people they wanted to be, instead of conforming to what everyone else thought?'

'But they started travelling because they hated all this.' She sounded defeated, not like the Kez he'd come to know. And respect. And like. And love a little.

'For themselves maybe. That doesn't mean they thought you should do it. Unless you wanted to. Is that what you still want?' And that was the question. What did she really want? 'And you said they were packing in the travelling anyway, so they can't have hated it that much. Maybe everything has its day, maybe they thought it was time to move on too.'

'But they didn't expect me to come back as well.'

'No, they expected you to do what was right for you. Did you ever tell them that you wanted to stand still for a bit?'

'I didn't know until….' She looked up at him. Clear hazel eyes with a touch of hurt. 'Why are you trying to stop me going, what's it to you anyway? I thought you wanted me to go.'

He had done. But he wasn't sure that this was true now. And was that because he didn't trust Simon, or was it just because he didn't want her to go?

'I don't want you to go for the wrong reasons.'

She gave a short laugh. 'You mean with another man?'

'Kez, don't try and wind me up.'

'So, what are the right reasons?'

'Because you want to, because it's right for you.'

'Well this place isn't right for me, is it? I don't know anything about horses or anything else you do here. According to you all I've done is learn how to make the horses belt around the arena.'

'That was a joke.'

'Funny.'

'Don't let him get to you, Kez, he doesn't know anything.'

'And you do?' She surveyed him with a distance in her gaze, a gap between them that he wanted to fill. 'What do you know about me? Oh, yeah you know what I'm like in bed, you know how to turn me on.' She shook her head as though she was working something out. 'Simon can look after me, he'd never let me down.'

'You can't know that.'

'No, I can't. But at least he wants to try. You've always had someone there for you, you've got this place, a job, and friends even if you don't want them. You haven't got a clue what being me is like.'

'And you'd just pack in everything you want, just run away like that?'

'You did. You ran away from your job and your family.'

'I didn't run away, I moved on to something I wanted to do. Something better.' But had he just run, had he given up because he couldn't face up to the truth, couldn't work out how to solve it? Had he just taken the easy route out?

'You had a fucking family, you had everything and just dumped it, so how can you tell me what to do?'

'It was my choice.'

'And maybe being with Simon is my choice, maybe it's better than being here pretending to be something I'm not.' But she didn't sound like she meant it.

He didn't want to lose her, didn't want her to widen that gap, build a barrier between them. Not yet. And he didn't want her to go with a man who seemed intent on scaring her into submission. 'He's trying to scare you.'

'And what if it's working?'

113

'You're tougher than that.' Right now she didn't look tough. She looked like a little girl lost; the first time he'd seen a real chink in her armour. The first time he'd seen doubt. And he didn't know what he wanted to do more, hold her or go and kick the shit out of the guy who'd just tried to rock the boat. No, not tried, he'd succeeded. 'Come here.' He pulled her from her chair, nearer, so that she sat straddled across his knee. He held both her hands. 'Why did you come here, Kez?'

'I had a plan.' She concentrated on their hands, fiddled for a moment then looked up at his face. 'I needed something after they'd gone.'

'What was in the plan?' If he kept her talking long enough she might forget about Simon, forget about taking the easy way out.

'To sort out a proper job for the first time in my life, learn something. But—'

'No buts. And?'

'Settle down in one place, make some friends. I just want to be normal, James. I want to feel like I've got something, someone.' She'd stopped fidgeting. 'I want to be a part of something. I'm never going to be clever or sophisticated, but I can be normal, can't I?'

He pulled her hands up so that he could kiss her cold knuckles slowly until she stopped resisting, until she gave a little, her arms loosened, relaxed. 'You are so much better than sophisticated or clever.' He released her hands, cradled her small elfin face, ran his thumbs along her cheekbones. He closed the distance between them so that he could touch her lips with his. Down by the river he'd wanted her so badly it had shocked him; he'd been glad of the interruption, glad of an excuse to run away. But now he didn't care. He just wanted to touch her, to taste her, to hold her. Before she ran. Before it was too late. 'Don't run scared, Kez.' He wrapped the long, dark silken hair around his hand, gently pulled back so that her neck was exposed. He slowly leant in so that he could smell her sweet scent, closer so that he could taste the saltiness, closer still so that his lips could tease at the soft skin until she sighed. 'Don't go backwards, you deserve more than that.'

'Make me want to stay.' She murmured.

He sucked gently, took in the taste of her. 'What do you want?'

'I want you to take control, I don't want to have to think any more. You can make it all go away.'

'Only you can do that, Kez.' He ran his tongue along her jawbone, felt her head drop further back. He couldn't make her happy, couldn't make it go away, but he wanted to make her stop and think before running. He didn't know why, and he didn't want to stop long enough to question it.

He lifted her onto the edge of the table, undid her jeans, never letting his gaze wander from those wanting eyes. There was a time for playing it slow, a time for building the anticipation, but this wasn't it. He stripped the tight jeans from her, pulled her knickers with them and then his fingers were on her sweet damp pussy. She was ready, gasping the moment he touched her. More needy than she'd never been, and as he slid inside her she moaned, wrapped her legs around him and her eyes clouded over with tears.

'It's okay to cry.'

'I'm scared.'

'Shush, I've got you.' He pulled her hips closer, kissed each eyelid in turn, pushing deeper inside and she wrapped herself around him like she was never going to let go. He put one hand behind her head, then pulled her close so that he could feel the damp wetness against his chest and their bodies rocked together in a slow, languorous dance until he felt her muscles tighten, until her fingernails dug into his shoulders and then he let go. He let himself fill her, and he felt drained, as though he'd worked all day long and there wasn't anything in him left to give. Then he picked her up, carried her back to the small bedroom that she called hers and lay down on the bed with her and felt like crying himself.

Kezia put out a hand and there was nothing but fresh air and rumpled sheets. Six a.m. and he'd stolen away. She'd hoped he could make her want to stay, but he couldn't. He'd done the very opposite. This convinced her that staying was the last thing in the world she should do.

She glanced towards the window, at the early-morning sun already filtering its way gently through the trees. Another fine day in paradise, as they say. She rolled out of bed, went over and stood at the window, clutching on to the window sill. James had made her forget, for a little while, but nothing had changed, nothing had gone away. And if Simon had really meant that they were after her, that it wasn't safe to be here then she'd be a fool to stay.

She'd honestly thought that it was all over, that they wouldn't have any interest in her now that they'd made an example of her parents. But she'd been kidding herself – she knew what Simon had been hinting at. Maybe he knew something she didn't, maybe they'd already been asking round, wanting to tie up loose ends. They must think she'd seen something, known something, that she was a threat. A small sliver of ice rolled around inside her and found a place to rest in her chest.

Simon had found her easily enough, so why shouldn't they? And what if they burned this little bit of heaven down? And for what? She was kidding herself that she was only here to start a new life. That was how it had started out at first, but it was different now.

Now she was here because of James. Staying because of him. She wasn't going to kid herself. She'd fancied the pants off him from the moment he'd appeared in the dimly lit yard, so dark and mysterious. His magnetic pull had drawn her into liking him, the real him rather than hating the man he pretended to be.

She'd been fooling herself that staying was the right thing to do. She meant nothing to him. Well nothing beyond being a good pupil. He didn't really care, didn't want any ties, anyone relying on him. He wasn't interested in the things she craved. Her clinging to him was no better than the way Simon was trying to hang on to her. Desperate. Unwanted. And she had clung to him last night, probably scarring him for life.

Yeah, well it would have all been over soon anyway, if it wasn't already. He'd have got bored of her pestering, moved on to something better. Marie and Dan would be back and she'd just be part of the fixtures and fittings. And not a particularly valuable part.

So why risk bringing trouble here? Why risk this place when she really had no reason to stay? Better to walk away now, then everything would go on being hunky-dory here for James and Marie, and she could just start over again somewhere else. Try again.

She bit the inside of her lip and the sharp sting was good. She wasn't going to pretend; she didn't really want to walk away. She liked it here, it almost felt like home, whatever that was meant to feel like. Giving it up, walking away was the last thing she wanted to do. Because for a moment she'd felt like this could be it; this could be the place to start again. And it was easy for him to say that she should stick with it. He'd never understand her. She needed people, wanted people and if she stayed here just to be with him, if she got any more involved she'd end up feeling even lonelier than she had been before.

And Simon had made her face up to it. He'd scared her into taking a step back and realising she was kidding herself, being a fool, as always.

She took one last look out of the window then dug a clean t-shirt and jeans out of her rucksack and started shoving her few other belongings into it. She'd checked the map on her mobile phone. If she walked the six or so miles into the village she could get a cab or hitch a ride to the railway station. She'd be out of his hair, which, after all was what he wanted, and soon no one would ever know she'd been here.

There was no sign of him when she padded down the stairs, shoes in her hands just in case. He'd be mucking out the stables, out of earshot. She took one last glance around then sneaked out of the back door. There was one open field to cross, and no sign of James, and then a post and rail fence to clamber over before she hit the lane.

A small pang of disappointment hit her as she let go of the rail. She didn't want him to see her, didn't want him to try and stop her, to be angry at her. She didn't want him to know she'd gone until she was miles away and it was too late. But it would have been nice to have had one last look at him, one more lingering look so she could imprint him on her memory. One more look because she knew she'd never see him again.

She glanced across the fields, her eye drawn to the chestnut in the distance who she could swear half lifted his head. Bugger. She'd liked it here. She'd more than liked him. She'd even liked his friggin' stroppy moods.

She settled the guitar more comfortable on her shoulder and tried to shake the thoughts out of her head. It would be daft to stay. Stupid. More than stupid. There would be somewhere else, somewhere better. Somewhere she was meant to be. And moping about here a second longer wasn't going to solve anything.

## Chapter 10

James glanced around the kitchen on his way towards the staircase. No sign of her. Not even the normal empty coffee cup or little pile of crumbs she always seemed to leave when she had toast. They'd be scattered over the table, then while she was chattering away she'd push them together into a neat little pile; a habit he'd not even thought about until she skipped doing it.

He'd expected her to turn up in the yard before he'd finished mucking out the stables, full of her normal cheeky asides, but she hadn't. And it hadn't seemed quite the same without her chattering away in his ear. It was quiet. Too quiet. Which was a turn up for the books.

True, he'd left her hours ago because he'd needed space. Last night's sensual lovemaking and the way she'd gently broken down in his arms had rattled him. And he didn't like being rattled. He didn't want to be relied upon and he didn't want her problems. He didn't want all the shit that came crashing in when you started to share more than just your bodies. But he didn't like her not being there beside him either. There was a space. And he'd been edgy, waiting for her to turn up and annoyed with himself for being like that. Christ, he was acting like some lovesick teenager.

He'd got used to the way she prattled on, the way she wound him up and made him laugh. Yup, she made him laugh, which

119

was another thing he hadn't been that keen on. He paused at her door, not sure whether to intrude or not. After all, who could blame her if she was pissed with him for doing an early-morning disappearing act?

Maybe she didn't want him there. He tapped on the door, and it made a strangely echoing noise that he didn't like. He only hesitated for a second, then swung the door open. And he knew. The bed was neatly made. The curtains open. But there was no rucksack. No guitar. No sign that Kez had ever existed. And if it hadn't been for the dull ache that hit him in the chest he would probably have believed she hadn't.

She'd walked.

She'd left this place. Left him.

Gone back to that scumbag with his barely veiled threats.

He stared at the bed. The bed that he'd been in only hours before. He'd been fucking right, you just gave a little and it all came crashing down. He'd served his purpose, given her a roof over her head, entertained her and shagged her to sleep. And now she'd moved on, without even a thank you and goodbye.

He slammed the bedroom door shut, then put the brakes on. He didn't do flying off the handle now. Since being here he'd found the person he wanted to be; even tempered, unemotional, eenjoying each day for what it was. No expectations and no getting involved. And now he was letting someone get to him. He gritted his teeth in frustration, could feel the pulse in his temple throbbing with something he didn't want.

Damn it, and damn her. Why the hell she was getting to him like this he didn't know. He hadn't wanted her here in the first place. And she had old simple Simon to look after her now. She didn't need him, had never needed him, which, if he was honest, had been part of the attraction.

He found himself back in the kitchen and it suddenly seemed too big and too empty. He wasn't in the mood for exercising the horses, he'd probably work out his anger on them and he didn't want to do that. So to hell with it, he'd do something he hadn't done in the morning for years. He'd head up to the pub in the village and if not drown his sorrows he'd do a damned good job of hammering his frustrations into touch. And when he'd purged her from his mind he'd come back and spend the rest of the summer how he'd always intended. On his own. In peace.

'Not seen you around for a while James, thought you were shut up for the summer?'

James didn't mind the landlord at the pub, Steve. He was easy going, never pried and hadn't even raised an eyebrow when they'd brought sex to the stables. And he was Roisin's brother, which helped.

'I was left behind to feed the horses.' He nodded at the pump for the local bitter.

'Pint?'

'Please.' If he hit the shorts now he'd be slaughtered by lunchtime.

'You've had that slip of a girl keeping you company, have you?'

James raised an eyebrow and the other man laughed. 'You think you can keep a secret in this place? No chance.' He pulled the pint slowly and James wished he'd hurry up, and shut up. 'She was here this morning looking for a ride.'

'Ah.'

'Heading back home was she?'

Okay, correction, maybe he did sometimes pry. 'Something like that, Steve.' He handed the money over for the drink, grabbed it and headed for the benches that made up the beer garden. Steve followed him. He was bored, no doubt. This had to be one of the quietest pubs in the country.

'She seemed like a nice girl.'

'One of Marie's waifs and strays.' He knocked back the drink, which hadn't been part of the plan and handed the empty back to the bemused Steve.

'She seemed taken with you.'

Yeah, taken enough to do a runner without even leaving a Dear John.

'James?'

'What?'

'Nothing. Except…'

'I thought you said nothing?'

'They aren't all like Chloe, you know.'

James wondered just how long Kez had been here, just how much she'd said.

'You don't need to chase them all away.'

'I didn't chase this one.' He patted the other man on the shoulder. 'This one made sure she didn't hang around long enough.' So much for a quiet drink.

~

Even walking at what, for him, was a slow pace, he was back at the riding school by midday. The motorbike was just inside the gate, still warm. It was tempting to kick it, but he didn't. Instead, he kicked himself for not chaining up the gate.

What the hell was Simon back here for? Back to pick something up that Kez had forgotten? There was no sign of Kez, though, when he tracked down Simon, staring vacantly across the fields.

'What do you want?'

The man turned and James resisted the urge to hit him. He was blond, tanned golden and slightly overweight. Too much good living, too little work. James remembered those days. Days he would never go back to.

'Where is she?' The voice was mainly city boy, with a slight tinge of accents he'd picked up on his travels. But it was the drawl in the background that wound him up. A self-confident 'I always get what I ask for' edge.

'Who?' He said the word before it clicked in his brain, Simon didn't know. She wasn't with him. She'd not run away to be with someone else, she'd just run away. Which was Kez all over. Make a decision and do it. She could do anything, she just didn't always realise. He suddenly realised he was smiling and Simon was looking uneasy.

'Stop fucking about. You know who.'

'If you're talking about Kezia, then, actually, I don't know where she is. I'm not her keeper.'

'She's got to come with me.'

'Looks like she's got other ideas.' Okay it was childish, but if she wasn't prepared to hang around here, he was glad she wasn't with Simon. He felt like he'd won the consolation prize.

'If you don't tell me—'

'What?' He laughed. 'What are you going to do? Leave her be, mate, she's not interested.' Being called 'mate' by the smarmy git yesterday had irritated him. Using it now was just cheap point-scoring, but he didn't care. He turned, headed for the house. He needed to get away before he lost his temper and manhandled the man back to his crappy motorbike. He took a breath, steadied himself. Simon might be slightly bigger, but it was flab and bluster. He'd been playing a game of year out and manual labour, and never lifted a finger. James knew the type. They weren't worth even thinking about. The only thing that needled him about this one was that Kez had fallen for him. And that for some reason he didn't want to leave her alone. And it wasn't affection. He was damned sure of that.

The man took a step or two after him, he heard the crunch of gravel. Simon hesitated, then seemed to think better of it and turn around. It was only when he heard the motorbike kick into life that he breathed normally again.

'Have you been drinking?'

'Yes, Marie. I've been drinking.' He'd not spoken to Dan or Marie for days, and now she was ringing, the one evening that he'd decided to make friends with the whisky bottle.

'Is Kezia there?'

Even well on the way to drunk he could hear the suspicion in her voice. 'Nope, she's flown the nest.'

'James.'

'Don't "James" me.' He tipped another measure of the amber liquid into the glass, sloshed the contents slowly around, watching it cling to the sides. 'This Simon guy came calling and,' he'd keep the explanation simple, 'she upped and went.'

'Just like that? With him?'

From the sharp note in her voice Marie hadn't exactly taken to the blondie. 'Nope.'

'Not with him?'

'No, isn't that what I just said?'

'Good.' There was a long pause.

'I thought she'd gone with him, but he came poking his nose around a couple of hours ago, ready to do the knight in shining armour bit and drag her away from my evil clutches.'

'Ha, some knight. I met him. He was a bit of a slime ball. I don't get why she was seeing him at all, really. He didn't seem her type, but it just seemed to be light between them, a bit of fun. Maybe he had hidden talents.' Her voice was dry, like she didn't believe it.

'Marie?' He took another gulp of the fiery liquid, let it burn its way down his throat. Didn't want to think about the guy's talents, hidden or otherwise. 'Is there a point to this call?'

'Oh yeah, sorry. I was trying to get hold of Kezia, really.'

'She's got a mobile.'

'I know.' She sighed. 'We're not all as stupid as you imagine, Jimmy boy. I've tried and I think it's probably dead.'

'Probably.' Though what it had to do with him he couldn't imagine. 'So, what am I supposed to do about it? I told you, I don't do babysitting.'

'Just how much have you had to drink?'

'Enough. Not that's it's any of your business. You're my boss, not my mother.' He had a horrible suspicion that he was behaving like some spoiled kid who had had their sweeties taken away.

'Fine.' Okay, he'd riled her now.

'I'm sorry.' And he was. He didn't normally take his angst out on other people, not that he knew why he was so pissed off. It had been a girl, the good times, now she was gone. Just how he liked it. 'If I see her I'll tell her you're after her.' Not that he was going to see her again. Something told him that she'd made her mind up this wasn't the place for her, so she wouldn't be back.

'Well, actually it's the police who've have been trying to get hold of her. David rang Ro, and she told him to try me—'

'David? As in PC Thomas?'

She laughed. But it sounded forced. In a village like this one it seemed that everyone knew everyone else's business, and considered everyone else a friend. It made sense in this place that if the local bobby couldn't get hold of someone at the riding school then he'd try ringing Roisin or Marie. 'It must be about her parents, and you're sure you don't know where she is? It doesn't sound like her to just disappear without even telling you where she was going.'

Well, she had this time. 'You don't know what they wanted?'

'He didn't say, look—' There was a trace of irritation in her voice, like he'd mislaid a prized possession. He had a horrible feeling there was a lecture heading his way.

'Stop there.' He closed his eyes. 'Email me with absolutely everything you know about her, and I mean everything. Then give me until lunchtime tomorrow. I'll try and find her.'

'You're a gem.'

'No, I'm not.' *I'm a stupid idiot who just let her go when she needed someone more than ever.* And he was too bloody selfish to show her that he cared at all, even a tiny bit. Yeah, he'd made love to her – and it had been more like making love than anything he'd felt in a long time. But she'd known he wouldn't be there for her. And he'd got up and gone before she'd stirred. Left her to wake up alone and worry. 'I'll find her.'

'Can you let David know? I'll put his number on the email.'

'Won't 999 do?'

'James.' But there was a trace of her normal good humour returning. He dropped his mobile back on the table and waited for the email.

It came within seconds, which meant she didn't know much more about Kez than he did.

He clicked it open, nursing his nearly empty glass in one hand. And he'd been right. A picture of Kez and her parents that somehow had got into Marie's hands, a copy of her passport, which Marie must have taken to check her out before offering her a job, and a few details about where she'd been before she turned up in Capri, what she did while she was there and a picture of her and Simon laughing together like they hadn't got a care in the world.

He snapped the laptop lid down and shut his eyes as a sudden yearning reached out and grabbed him unawares. He might be bad for her, he might not be able to solve her problems or look after her like she so obviously wanted. But he could help her, he had to go after her – and it was nothing to do with the promise he'd just made Marie. He wanted to see her again.

Shit. The passport. He opened up the laptop again, waiting while it laboriously edged its way back into life, connected to the wireless. She'd been born in the UK, she'd told him that much. And there it was, town and country of birth. He stared. He didn't know Kez well, but he knew her well enough to know that if she could, she'd head home. And right now, this town named on her passport, this place she hardly knew – if at all – was the nearest she'd got to a home.

His head shouted out a warning to him when the early-morning light woke him up. He closed his eyes again and waited for the sharp jab in his temples to go away. It was an overload warning and he'd forgotten it could feel so bad. Whisky might be good for the soul, but it was damned lethal for the brain.

The pain eased and he sat up cautiously, which seemed to work. Great. He had the horses to feed and turn out before he could head off for the day, so he'd either end up feeling sick as a dog or the fresh air would work its miracle cure.

A cold shower helped, the water pounding down on the tense muscles in his shoulders washed away the grimy alcohol-tinged sweat. But when he went down into the empty kitchen some of the tension came back. It shouldn't. She was never in the kitchen when he got up this early, but it was knowing that she wouldn't be there later either.

The black coffee kick-started his body – if not his muggy brain, which still felt like it had been infiltrated by zombies going around in meaningless circles in search of something that wasn't there. Which was pretty much how the rest of him felt once he started to work in the yard.

By the time the last horse had been turned out he'd almost switched into normal mode. They'd sensed his mood, his lack of concentration and played up accordingly. Spooking at invisible monsters and seeing craters by the gateways they walked through every day. Horses, he decided grimly, were a bit like women. If you weren't tuned in they knew it. And if you didn't change they'd lead you a merry dance. But he did like the horses, fickle as they could be. He gave Red a slow stroke down his elegant nose, steadying him for a second before letting him loose. The horse paused, then threw his head up and wheeled around before cantering off down the field with his tail held high, as though the grapes of wrath were upon him. James smiled, despite his bad mood. No wonder Kez had picked the bloody horse out – they were two of a kind, wanting your attention one minute, proving they were fiercely independent the next. And also that no one was going to change them. He gave the gate a rattle to make sure it was shut. No use shutting the stable door after the horse had bolted. Ha. Fine time to come out with earthy snippets like that.

He checked his watch. Steve would be up and about now, and

he wanted a quick chat before he hit the road. The car keys were in the kitchen so he grabbed them, drove out of the gate and made sure he wound the chain securely around it and snapped the heavy padlock shut. By his reckoning, Simon wouldn't risk dropping by again, but he wasn't chancing it.

'I'm honoured. Two visits in as many days.' Steve carried on with his sweeping of the pathway that led up to the pub. 'You look a bit rough around the edges.'

James hoped his smile was more normal than it felt.

'Guess it wasn't my one pint that did that to you.'

'At a rough guess I'd put it down to the half bottle of whisky. You said Kez stopped by?'

'She did.'

'Did she say where she was heading?'

Steve looked like he wanted to ask questions, but had decided against it. 'She wanted a lift to the station. I called her a taxi.'

'She didn't say anything else?'

'You're not just asking out of interest are you?'

'Nope. I think you've done that path to death.'

Steve laughed and stopped his sweeping.

'It's important. I need to find her and her mobile's off, or more likely dead.'

'Give me a minute, I'll give Mike a call. She might have said something to him. You know, the cabbie.'

His gut was already telling him where she'd gone. A small town in the suburbs of Manchester. The one named on her passport. But his gut hadn't been that reliable lately, or he hadn't been listening.

'Manchester.' Steve had appeared at the door of the pub again. Phone in hand. 'She was asking about trains to Manchester.'

'Cheers.' He was right. 'Hey mate you missed a bit, there.' He pointed at the edge of the path and got a swipe of the broom from Steve, which just missed.

'Piss off.' His face switched to serious. 'James, she's not in some kind of trouble is she?'

'Not sure. I'll let you know when I find her.'

'You're going to Manchester?'

'I am. And Steve,' he turned back as he reached the road, 'if some blond guy turns up asking questions don't say anything, yeah?'

'Sure. You know me, my lips are sealed.'

'Landlords tend to have leaky seals.'

He laughed good-naturedly. 'Bugger off before you get a leaky seal or two.'


Once he hit the main road, it was an easy run. 'A' roads and motorways all the way, the type of roads he never drove on these days. Tension started to curdle in his stomach, the tightness that had become as much a part of his life as breathing. Fear, anticipation, the incessant feeling that today would be worse than yesterday. Tomorrow would hurt even more. The pressure had built day on day, the boredom of work, the mixture of anticipation and dread that increased as the time crept on and on, nearer to the time when they'd head home. When it would be she and him.

The dull ache in his jaw grew, until he realised he was gritting his teeth. He took a deep breath. Forcing his hands to relax on the steering wheel, he eased his teeth apart. It had been over for a long time. Too long for him still to be thinking about it. It was just a road.

He settled into the seat and relaxed his shoulders. Kez had accused him of running away, and she'd been right. He was more of a coward than she'd ever been. And what had it been about? Nothing really, a bad relationship. An affair that he'd thought was right at the start, but had turned out wrong. He'd been determined to bury the past, bury it as deeply as he could. He'd told her 'some things are better left in the past' and he'd meant it. And yet things wouldn't stay where he'd tried to shove them. 'You shouldn't put them there until you understand them' she'd said and she was probably right. He'd never really thought about what had happened, never questioned why it had hit him the way it had. He'd just run away. He double-checked with the directions on his phone, then signalled and peeled off the motorway onto the 'A' road that would take him to Prestbury.

And he'd hassled her for giving up, running back to what she knew. Who the hell was he to judge her? He'd taken the easy option, the easy life. She hadn't.

He suddenly realised that the traffic had thinned and he'd slowed down. What if he couldn't find her? What if he could? He didn't know which he dreaded more.

The town was smaller than he expected – more of a village. A couple of minutes and he'd driven through, out of the other end. He pulled into a driveway, turned around and headed more slowly back into the centre of the village again.

He'd somehow expected a suburban sprawl, the type of place he could imagine someone running away from. The type of urban hell that her parents could have grown tired of, full of noise and dirt. Rat race. But this wasn't. It was small, picturesque, the type of place he'd been brought up in himself. A church, restaurants, a few chic shops, a scattering of trees and well-kept gardens. Luxury cars that had been polished to within an inch of their lives.

Maybe they'd just got bored and wanted a bit more excitement; some people were born wanderers, others just wanted to sit still. He drew up outside a pub and sat for a minute before turning the ignition off. If she was here, he'd find her. That was a certainty. He half smiled to himself. The town was not a good place to hide if that had been her intention, but a good place to feel like you could belong. He pushed open the door of the vehicle and got out. If she wasn't here then he didn't know where to look next. All he'd worked on was his instinct that she'd act like a homing pigeon, but apart from the little bit she'd told him, and the stark facts in her passport, he hadn't got a damned thing to go on.

He locked the Land Rover up and stretched, edging the kinks out of his spine. It hadn't been a long journey, but he'd been wound up like a coiled spring, and he felt like he'd been run over. Repeatedly. He could start at the pub, which was where he'd have headed. But she wouldn't. And she'd already been here a day, if she was here at all.

He leant against the vehicle, glanced up and down the high street, hands shoved deeply in his pockets, catching some air. The church, a place where anyone could feel like they belonged. If there was one place in this village that would draw her in it would be the church.

You couldn't miss it, a stately symbol of grandeur that was the centre of any village and which had been around as long as this place had. He paused at the lych gate; if she didn't want to see him it was fine. He'd pass on the message, hit the road and go back to the life he loved. End of story. He took a step in through the already -pen gates, the pathway mottled with the sunlight filtering through the trees.

She didn't take much finding.

He followed the path around the edge of the church, turned a corner and she was there, hands clasped in her lap, dark hair masking her face. But even though he knew his footsteps were virtually silent, she looked up, saw him, before he could decide whether to speak or not. He just wanted to watch her. Work her out. She didn't move, just looked and waited. Which was fair enough; he was the one that had turned up without an invite.

'Nice place.' Stupid comment, but it was the first thing that came into his head. Her face was ultra-serious, not a hint of a smile. But she didn't look angry that he'd tracked her down. Or curious about why he was there.

'They probably should be buried here. What do you think?' She didn't ask why he was there, how he'd found her. 'Do you think they'd want to be?' Her attention was back on the churchyard in front of her.

'As good a place to call home as any.' He covered the ground between them and sat next to her on the wooden, green-tinged bench. 'If I had to stop, then I'd be happy here I think. They might like to come home, finish the journey where they started.'

'Full circle.' She stared ahead, at the regimented gravestones.

'Did they live here for long?'

'Dunno.' She half-turned her head and that brown-green gaze hit him full on. 'I don't know that much about them really, we didn't have photo albums or cosy chats about the past. It was all about living in the present. I never had time to ask. It was too late. James?' He waited. 'I'm tired. I'm so fucking tired of moving on.'

'I know.' He let himself close the gap between them, let himself put an arm around her and she just seemed to cave in, leaning against him, her soft body moulding against his like it belonged there. Her head rested on his shoulder. 'You didn't have to go.'

'I did.' He could hardly hear her small voice.

'Why?'

She gave a heavy sigh and it rippled through her body and through his. 'I didn't want anything to happen. It's too nice there for me to spoil it.'

'Nothing was going to happen, Kez.'

'You don't know that. Simon said they'd come, the people who....'

'He didn't actually say that, did he?' He kneaded gently at her arm, if they had come he could have looked after her. But he'd never told her that, had he?

'That's what he meant. He knew about what happened. He tracked me down, so why shouldn't they?'

'You didn't tell him where you were?'

'No. Why would I tell him?'

'He didn't have to do any tracking; all he had to do was talk to Marie. He was just trying to make you go back to him, realise you needed him.'

'But I don't. I was never going to go back.' She shifted uneasily.

'But why would anyone be after you?' He'd asked himself that question over and over as he'd driven to find her. Okay, she might be right that someone had killed her parents for not playing the game – not giving in to their demands to drop it. These people had lost their stash of whatever drugs they'd been trying to move across the border, but Kez's parents were just the mules. They'd never seen the people who had planted the drugs, were never supposed to – there was no line back to the traffickers. So what interest would they have in the daughter who knew nothing? Chasing her across the channel would be dangerous and pointless. Old, simple Simon was just planting fear, stirring up doubts and ghostly images in places they had no right to be.

'Simon warned me, he'd come across things like that before,' he said. He told me to stay close to him, stay with him and he'd make sure I was safe. Then when I came here, he kept texting to say he thought they were looking, that people had been asking questions. Look, I'm not going back to him, okay? That's not why I left. Don't look at me like that.' He hadn't thought he was looking like anything. 'I know you think it's all rubbish, that I never know what I'm talking about.'

'Come on, that's not fair. I've never accused you of talking rubbish.' The scepticism must have shown on his face, because her shoulders had tightened. 'I just can't see why they'd come here looking for you, what would they gain?'

'But if they are after me... James I don't want them damaging your place. Let's face it, you didn't want me there—'

'I never said—' He'd never said he did, never said he didn't.

'You didn't want me there and so why risk trouble? I'm better off starting again somewhere else. Anyhow.' She looked him straight on again. 'What are you doing here?'

'Marie's been trying to get hold of you.'

'Oh.' She caught at her lower lip with tiny white teeth. 'I just switched my phone off, I was sick of the texts from Simon. Why?'

'The police have been trying to get hold of you. They wouldn't say why, but I thought it might be important.'

So, he hadn't come because he missed her, because he needed her like she needed him. He'd come to pass on a message, to tell her the police wanted to talk. Kez was hit by a sudden feeling of despondency. For a brief second then, her hopes had shot up. Which was bloody silly. She was right; he turned up and was capable of making her feel even lonelier than she'd ever been in the past. He was like some mirage in the desert. Raising your hopes, then disappearing into the blue before you got your hands on him. It would have been better if he'd never tracked her down, except some little part of her heart had lurched the moment she saw him, and even knowing he was only playing postman she still couldn't make herself wish he wasn't here.

'Here.' He was holding out his phone. 'Call them.'

She didn't really want to. Didn't really want any more questions, she just wanted it to be over.

'You need to.'

What did he know about what she needed? She took it reluctantly. He'd already got the number up, so all she had to do was press the call button.

'Do you want me to leave you to it?'

She shook her head and put her hand in the open one he had on his knee. Pressed 'call.'

They said they needed her to call in the station in person, with her passport. Confidential information.

'I'll take you. Come on, where did you stay last night? We'll go and grab your stuff.'

'You don't need to.'

'Kez.' He squeezed her hand a bit tighter, twisted his body a bit so that he was looking straight at her. 'I want to.'

'I'll be fine.'

'You will, yes. With me.'

He stood up, taking her with him, seeing as he still had a hold of her hand. So she had a choice; use her superior strength to get away (ha! some chance) or have a screaming fit so he'd let go.

Or go along with it. And she actually wanted to go along with it. Except it was one step deeper into a disaster zone.

'Okay.' *Silly girl.* 'But, you're going to give me a lift back here after, as well?'

'You're kidding, look there's no reason to—'

'Chill. I was kidding.' He slapped her bum with his free hand and for the first time smiled. His toe-curling, stomach-twisting smile that was no good at all for her.

Nor was sharing a space in his Land Rover.

'You didn't have to settle up at the pub. I could have sorted the bill.'

'You can pay me back.' He put a hand on her knee, even more not good. 'In one way or another.' A devilish wink that was more than not good, along with a squeeze that sent a shiver of recognition between her thighs.

The motorway was quiet, a light trickle of mid-week, mid-afternoon traffic that they kept pace with. She wasn't in any hurry, she wanted to put off the arriving bit, and James seemed to be thinking the same. They were just cruising along steadily until the inevitable exit loomed close and soon they were bumbling along the narrow lanes that she'd become quite fond of.

It would have been nice if the journey had taken longer. Nice to be close to James and nice not to have to think about what came next.

He snatched the handbrake on as they pulled up outside the small police station.

'Will it be open at this time? I mean, we could come back—'

'He'll be there, he knows we're coming, he's waiting to talk to you.'

'You can wait out here for me if you like.'

'No way, Kez. I'm coming in.'

'I don't need you to.'

He grinned, moved in close, kissed her lightly. 'Yes, you do, darling.'

'It might be something and nothing.'

'It might.' He was out and opening her door before she had a chance to object. 'Come on, move that pretty little butt of yours or I'll throw you over my shoulder and carry you in.'

'You wouldn't dare.'

'Dare?' His eyes had narrowed and he put both hands on her waist. 'Wouldn't I?'

'Okay, okay, let go, Tarzan.'

But as they walked up and pushed the door open, she was damned glad he'd got a hold of her hand. Damned glad she had something to hang on to.

# Chapter 11

'Hey, David. You run off your feet as normal?'

'Non-stop here in this den of iniquity.'

Kezia stared at the PC. He was middle aged, but with youthful features, slightly thinning hair and he looked capable. Steady and capable; the type of man who could solve all your troubles. She hoped.

'And you must be Miss Martin? Sorry to have to ask,' he shrugged, as though such things were the bane of his life, 'but I need to see your passport.'

She rummaged in her rucksack, finally finding the battered, fading passport in the fourth pocket she tried. Well it had been the first one, but she'd missed it and searched everywhere else with trembling hands that had forgotten how to handle a zip.

'Great, thanks.' He gave it a fairly cursory look then handed it back. 'I'm PC Thomas, by the way. Call me David,' he gave James a look accompanied by a raised eyebrow, 'everyone else does.' He lifted the end of the counter. 'Come through, we can talk in the back.' He sat them down, then shuffled through the papers on his desk, which Kez suspected was for their benefit not his own. In a place like this there couldn't be much going on, there just couldn't be. Unless you counted lost dogs and reports of marriage tiffs as major incidents. 'Here we go.' He smoothed out what looked like a fax. 'Here, you can read it yourself.'

He pushed the paper towards her, and she pushed it on towards James. 'You read it. Please.'

'I love it when you say please.' He squeezed her knee, then took the sheet of paper. 'It's good, Kez.' There was a hint of relief in his voice that she couldn't miss. Up until now he'd done a bloody good job of acting Mr Cool, so she took a breath. Waited. Glad he was there. 'They've arrested someone, it says that you can make arrangements to bring them home, and,' he paused, as though he wasn't sure he should read the next bit.

'And?'

'They want to know the whereabouts of Simon Jacobsen.'

'Simon?'

'You know him?' The constable had taken the fax back and his tone had sharpened.

'He was here the other day.' James answered for her.

'Why do they want Simon?'

'I'll find out. Go home.' He'd stood up. No doubt it was the most exciting thing he'd had to do all year. 'Go home and I'll let them know he's been here so they can check out if he's left the country or not, and I'll try and find out why they want to talk to him. Okay? Right, I'll ring you at the stables.'

And they were ushered out faster than she thought possible. Obviously he was more efficient and assertive than she'd realised. She got in the Land Rover. The problem was, it meant she was heading back to the riding stables. With James.

A type of prison sentence, or should that be pleasure sentence? She gave an inward sigh that she guessed from the weird look he tossed her must mean it showed on her face.

'I don't want you to be on your own.'

'Makes a change from what you said when you found me hanging on to your gate the first time.'

'Yeah well, you did have a bit of the loony look about you.'

'Gee, ta. I always said you were a gent.'

'Can I just check something?'

'Check away.'

He swung up to the gate. Got out. Undid the padlock to beat all padlocks and unwound the chain before pushing open the gate and climbing back in.

He shoved the 4x4 into gear and drove into the yard, switching off the engine before turning to look at her. 'You didn't do a runner so you could meet up with the blond sex god?'

He must be joking. Nope, from the look on that dark face he wasn't. Zilch on the laughter front. 'Why would I run off to meet him when he said he'd come and pick me up? Duh.' Still no glimmer of the light fantastic, just the moody and broody. Which had its plus points.

'Why didn't you tell me you were going?'

'Says the man who shagged me senseless then disappeared at the crack of dawn.'

'I had to do the horses, you were tired.'

'Bollocks. Look, I'm not stupid, but what gives you the right to start quizzing me now, eh? You pissed off in the morning because you didn't want to face me getting all gushy and begging you for more. Fat chance. Sex god you might be, but Mr Stay With Me Forever you ain't. What makes you think I want anything more anyway?'

'Okay, I admit it, you're right, Miss Clever Clogs. Now can we quit the name-calling? I did get up because I didn't want a cosy chat. You scare me, Kez, don't you get that?'

'Me?' She laughed. 'I couldn't scare a mouse.'

'I'm not a mouse. Why didn't you say something? Didn't you trust me not to tell someone?'

'I trusted you, but,' she did trust him; it was her that had the problem, 'I didn't trust myself to go through with it if I hung about. I was scared, James. I like it here, but I didn't want them coming here and burning the place down.' Funnily, saying it out loud made it not quite as scary any more. Verging on silly rather than scary. But it had seemed real twenty-four hours ago. 'And let's face it, you couldn't really give a shit, we were just having a bit of fun. It's not worth risking all that just so we can carry on our,' she paused, *our what*? 'Frolic.' Stupid word, but the first one that seemed vaguely appropriate.

A hint of a smile played across those severe features. 'Frolic?' He raised an eyebrow.

'Okay, laugh at me.'

'So you went to stop the place getting burned down?'

'More or less. I just thought it was better to short-cut the frolic and do what was going to happen soon enough anyway. So, I ran away like the coward I am.'  ·

'You're not a coward, you're a damned sight braver than most people I know. Not many people would be prepared to just jack things in when it looked like what they were fighting for was about to happen, and start all over again.' He ran his hands over the steering wheel, and she watched, mesmerised, as his fingers played a silent tune. 'It took guts to walk away again.'

'If you don't try you won't know.'

'True.' He seemed to make a sudden decision. The tune stopped abruptly. 'I want to show you something.' He grabbed her ruck-sack out of the back, let her get the guitar herself and started off towards the house.

They'd just about got to the door when his mobile rang.

'It's for yo;, old Sherlock himself.'

'Sherlock?' She looked stupidly at the mobile he was holding out.

'Our village constable. Here, take it. Come on, don't deprive him of the chance to solve something.'

She wasn't sure she wanted to take the call, whatever she was depriving the PC of. She'd slept with Simon, she'd eaten and got slightly merry with him, she'd sat pillion on his bike and astride his body. And now someone was asking questions about him. It seemed slightly surreal. James had taken her look as a 'no' and taken the call himself. There were lots of 'I sees' and 'really?' and 'you don't say' and 'the bastard.' So she satisfied herself with slumping in the armchair and watching him. He was nice to watch. It was his perfect stillness – even when he was on the move, there was nothing stilted or rushed, he kind of held himself together, restrained and controlled. Panther-like. Which was a bit kinky. He had his hand tucked into his pocket, emphasising his lean hips, those long legs with a hint of muscle. He clicked the phone off, caught her staring.

'So, if you know you're safe here are you going to stay?'

'Who says I'm safe?'

'Me.'

'That's the last thing I'd call you, buster.'

'Marie will kick my butt if I let you escape again.'

'Is that all you're bothered about?'

'No.' He moved closer on silent feet. 'I'm bothered about you. Do you want to know what he said?'

'Do I need to?'

He had stooped down in front of her, one hand either side of her thighs and it was getting harder to breathe normally. 'I think so.' That gruff edge was creeping in, the one that made the hairs on the back of her neck prickle with awareness. 'They think Simon is one of the people that identifies possible mules. He's been doing it for a while now.'

'Oh.'

'He doesn't have anything to do with the drugs.' His thumbs brushed against her legs. 'Just plays the dumb tourist and makes friends, finds out where people are headed.'

'And sleeps with them?'

'I don't think that's part of the deal, no.'

'But he was so nice. He can't be involved, he can't go around killing people.'

'I don't think he does, he just makes easy money spotting people who are going in the right direction.'

'And then they sent him here after me?'

'David doesn't seem to think so, he says it wouldn't make sense, would make them traceable. I thinks Simon just wanted you back and thought playing the big protector might help.'

'But they don't know that.'

'They're pretty sure.'

'So nobody is interested in me?'

'I wouldn't say that.' He leaned in, kissed that sensitive spot on her neck. It would be so easy to just cave in, go along with it all again until this time he had got fed up of her. She cleared her throat. 'What was it you wanted to show me?'

He stopped the kissing bit then and went and got his laptop. He fired it up and fiddled a bit, then pulled her over to sit next to him on the floor.

The woman in the pictures was tall and the word 'statuesque' fitted her like a glove. The red hair was straight as a die, the perfectly straight fringe hanging just above dark eyebrows, the line of her bob cut at an angle so that it mimicked the run of her high, well-defined cheekbones. Blue eyes stared defiantly out as though challenging the man behind the camera. Strong thighs were wrapped in black fishnet stockings, red and black suspenders snaked through skimpy knickers and her body was lovingly encased in a red and black corset threaded through with black satin ties. And across her body she held a whip, her fingers lightly closed around the end, as though she were caressing it.

Kez stared and didn't know whether the picture was enticing or frightening, which she guessed was probably the point. Scared or aroused. Take your pick.

'Chloe.' She hadn't realised she'd said it out loud until he gave a short laugh, right next to her ear, which made her jump because she'd been so fixated with the picture.

'Chloe indeed.' He flicked onto another picture. Chloe in soft focus, pink negligee, but still the same eyes, staring out. Dominating. Demanding attention.

'She looks scary.'

'She is.' He flicked onto the next image. More black leather, handcuffs.

'You were into the whole bondage scene?' She didn't really know what to call it, didn't really understand anything beyond what she'd read.

'Not really. It was a game for her, she didn't bother going the whole hog or believe in the whole dom/sub thing. She just liked playing, pushing the boundaries. Everything was a challenge, seeing how far she could go, how far I'd go. Every time we had sex it had to be different, more dangerous or she wasn't interested. But getting the next fix was an obsession and it got dangerous. It was like getting spanked; first time it was fun, a mild turn-on because it was different and then she wanted more pain to see if it was more of a high. She wanted to know which the bigger high was, the pain or the pleasure. I was young, naïve and I put her on a pedestal; she was confident, had no hang-ups about her body or what she wanted and that was some aphrodisiac. I totally trusted her with every bit of me.'

'And it was good?'

'At first. It was all about submission, though, one of us giving in to the other. When she was in charge you could see the thrill she got, it turned her on more than anything else having that power. In return for letting her get her thrills she'd eventually give me some back. And she got a thrill from being submissive too. She liked the pain, seeing how much she could cope with, seeing how much you were prepared to give her. I had to give her enough or she wouldn't let herself give in to the pleasure. I got to the point where I felt sick not knowing how far she'd go, and even though the sex at the end could be mind-blowing it became less and less important. The pain became the thrill for her; seeing how far she could push us both.'

James flicked on through the photographs. He'd never shown anyone, nor looked at them himself. And yet now he didn't feel the same stab of pain he'd anticipated. They were just dead pictures, lifeless. It hit him that he hadn't got a single picture that just showed Chloe as a happy, laughing human being. They were all sexual images, smoke and mirrors. Chloe used the camera in the same way she used people, to create an image.

She had an almost magnetic quality, the something that drew people in, even when they didn't want to be. And it wasn't just the suspenders, the fuck-me clothes. It was something deeper, like forbidden fruit. Chloe promised an experience that was bad for you.

'But you must have got something from it, learned something?'

He paused, he'd never thought of it that way. Learning from frustration and terror.

'You must have gained something?' Her voice was soft, as though she didn't quite believe it herself, but being Kez, she was trying to find a positive. Make it normal.

'Not to trust anyone?' Okay, he sounded bitter. He was bitter.

'Do you mean that?'

'I thought so.' He stopped. 'I'm not sure now.' And he wasn't.

'Maybe you were just too young, I mean she was older than you, you didn't know how to pick the right person to trust. I mean, it's a lottery isn't it? Life, love all that shit. But if you don't take a risk—'

'Then you don't lose.'

'Or win.'

'Clichéd.'

'But true.'

'Doesn't it bother you, seeing this stuff?' He'd thought she might be appalled, but he'd been hiding it too long, he wanted to let it go. Expose it. He'd been hiding it from himself as much as anyone else. What was it? If you can't see it, it can't exist?

'Well it's not exactly what I'm used to, but I mean, I know some people do it.'

He slowly closed the lid of the laptop, he'd seen enough of Chloe.

Showing the pictures had been one thing, but he had to tell her everything. She'd been right – he shouldn't bury things he didn't understand and right now he was trying like hell to understand what it had all been about. And at the end of the day, maybe Chloe had been a bit like him, needing to be in control, needing to prove she was top dog. And she did that by constantly daring him to go further. For her. He took a deep breath. 'My dad had sex with her, or rather she did with him.'

'What?'

'She gave my father a blow job and then told me about it when she was fucking me.'

'Your-?' She was open-mouthed, he knew without looking. He'd be open-mouthed too.

'He didn't know it was her.'

'How?'

'It was when we first met, before we went out together. I guess I'd been targeted as an up-and-coming confident idiot to add to her collection. All her Christmases came at once when she found out my father was a barrister: power, money, and experience, just what a girl like her wanted. He was her research project: a powerful man who was malleable when it came to sex.' He suppressed the inward shudder. They'd never been close, but no son wanted to think of his domineering father as a man with a kinky side. 'She told me the full story when she had me tied to the bed with a hard-on. I'm not quite sure whether I was supposed to break down or beat her up. At the end of the day it was just another tool in her armoury, I think, to stop me straying.' And he hadn't strayed, even though he'd started to hate her. 'She met him in a bookshop, one of those small private shops with dark corners, flicking his way through erotica. They were both so fucking upfront and blasé about everything that she just asked about his fantasies and before she knew it had a Wednesday afternoon slot to help him fulfil them. She flattered his ego I suppose.' He looked at Kez who was watching him like he'd grown two heads. 'Like she flattered mine.

Young stud; like father like son.'

'But you aren't. Like your father, I mean.'

'No.' He'd never wanted to be the sub. Being jumped on by a woman every now and again, well yeah, who would say no? Being made to beg for a beating? Not his style.

'But why would anyone do something like that? I mean, are you sure…'

'I think she did it so that she could goad me into losing my rag and hitting her properly. It was all about testing me, and testing herself.' More about her, he supposed looking back, what she could get away with, how it turned her on. Like an animal that's tasted its first blood and has to go back for more, just to test whether it's as good second time round.

'And did you?' It was a tiny whisper in the stillness. 'Did you hit her?'

'No, but I so very nearly did.' Even when he'd started to hate her in a way he didn't think he could hate another person, he couldn't lose his self-control. He hadn't wanted to, he'd just felt sad and sick inside, and known the game had lost its appeal. 'Then I met one of her exes who she'd done much the same to and it finally got through my thick skull that I was just a toy and if I didn't get out it would get worse.'

For a long time he'd hung on to the belief that she'd reach the end of the road in her little adventure. That they'd go back to affection rather than competition, lead a more normal life. Find something new to challenge them. But then he'd realised that this was the normal life she wanted.

She'd been clever, married him in a romantic rush that needed a special licence abroad, persuaded him that meeting the family should wait – that a secret spiced things up. And it had been easy, because there had been a gulf of disinterest. No reason for introductions. So he'd humoured her until he'd started to have doubts, and then she'd told him she already knew daddy.

He had been tempted to call her bluff, take her to the place they called home and watch the fireworks. He knew from his parents that marriage was an arrangement that required polite distances, and who you slept with and who you married weren't always the same thing as far as they were concerned. But why should he let Chloe destroy it? Or let his father destroy her? 'I think at the end of the day we knew fuck all about each other. I didn't know what made her tick, and she didn't give a shit about what did it for me. It was all psychological; blow you up then knock you down.'

'And she never thought you'd be able to walk away.'

'Suppose not, not on my own terms anyway. Except,' he let himself reach out, brush her hair behind one ear, 'I never quite walked away did I?'

'And have you now?' There was the slightest hint of a quaver in her voice, a quiver of tension that he loved to hear, that matched something deep in his body. They were in tune.

'I think so.'

She ran her tongue over her full lips. 'So you can bury it now.' Her hands were still clasped in her lap as though she daren't let go.

'Right now I want to frolic, and the only thing I'm interested in burying involves my cock and your pussy.'

He hardly noticed the little 'ooh.' He pushed her back so that she lay on the couch and she reached for the buckle of his belt as his hands closed on the waistband of hers. She grinned, tugged harder with frustration, her slender, cool hand wriggling its way into his jeans, closing around his aching cock. He gasped, closed his eyes. 'You're going to have to be damned careful what you do with that.'

She laughed, which made it worse. 'Safety catch off already is it?'

'Fully loaded, safety catch off.' He pulled away, stripping her jeans off as he moved and as he peeled his own t-shirt over his head she matched his movements. Tanned flat stomach, softly rounded breasts that moved with each breath she took. Christ, this was even harder than he thought it would be. She held her arms up, her eyes wide.

'If you don't give me some of that big hard cock that you've been teasing me with all afternoon right now I might have to come and get it.'

'Some?' He raised an eyebrow, but he knew the shake in his voice matched hers. 'You're getting all of it, like it or not.'

It was like coming home, sinking into Kez. Into that warm, slick channel that wrapped around and held him. 'I don't know whether I can hold it.' The second he was in he froze, not daring to move until he had at least some control over the urge to give two hard thrusts and come inside her. He took a deep breath, held onto her hips. Some, being the word.

'You can.' Her teeth were gritted and there was a fierce determination on her face. 'No way are you coming without me, mate.'

'You are just too bossy for your own good, woman.' It was getting better, the teenage urge to shoot his load had been squashed.

She was grinning up at him. 'You look like you're planning world domination.'

'Woman domination.' He grinned back. 'I'm reciting the Bible backwards.'

'Really?'

'No.' He let himself ease out of her, thrust all the way back in. She gasped. 'Can you do that bit again, please?'

'Ah the lady does know how to say please.'

'James?'

'Mmm.'

'Just shut up and fuck me.'

He wasn't quite sure how they ended up rolling off the couch and onto the floor; something to do with the way she was thrusting her hips up to match him, something about the way she was fighting to be on top. But he was lying on his back with her astride him, leaning back, holding his legs. Her small, perfect breasts jiggled, her slightly rounded stomach pulled flat and he could see where their bodies joined, how he eased in and out of her. He held onto her hips tight, added his thrusts to her own,

148

then he slipped his thumb between them, pressed against her clit and felt the shudder run through her. Her thighs tightened, then loosened, loosened as she sank against him and he sank deeper inside her and his aching balls were tightening. He moved his hand back to her hip, pulled her hard down as he forced himself up and came. Shooting hard inside her, the pulsing went on and on until it hurt. 'Fuck, Kez.' He could hardly breathe and felt light-headed. He closed his eyes, waiting for his body to slow and come back down to earth.

'I do believe you just have.' She giggled and rolled off. 'Fucked Kez, that is.'

'Funny.' He couldn't move. The lightest touch of her finger was on his chest, tracing circles in the hair. He covered it with his own, stopping the movement. 'You will stay, won't you?'

## Chapter 12

'I'd quite like you to fuck me down here, in the stables.'

'You would, would you? Well your wish is my command, just bend over while I put my pitchfork down.'

'I like that smell, the earthy wood shavings and hay smell,' she kept an eye on him in case he did put the pitchfork down, 'and the sweat.'

'You're a dirty girl.'

He was stripped to the waist, tiny beads of sweat on his brow and his chest and it probably shouldn't have been making her feel horny, but it was.

'Stop staring, woman.'

'I like staring. I'd quite like to be licking as well.'

'Stop it.'

'Or?'

He carried on mucking out. He wheeled the full barrow past her and she watched as he paused in the yard to swill his hand under the tap, and take a drink.

'God, you can be boring sometimes.'

He raised an eyebrow. 'And you—' He moved so fast she never saw it coming. One minute he was shaking his head at her, the next his hand had snaked around her waist and he'd pulled her to him, then yanked her off her feet and over his shoulder. 'You, can be a nuisance who needs teaching a lesson.'

'Stop it. Just stand still and put me down.' She pounded on his back with her fists and he never broke stride.

'Boring, my arse.'

'Okay I take it back, you're not boring.'

'Too late.' She tried kicking but he just clamped an arm down over her thighs and kept going.

'Where are you taking me?'

'You'll see.'

She gave up on the struggling, which was just making her hot and dragged a finger down his back instead, then she used her mouth. Sucking in the sweet saltiness of his skin. He grunted, but kept going.

'You need cooling down.' He stopped abruptly and before she'd even got her bearings properly he let her go. She slipped down his front, except her feet didn't hit the ground. They kept going. Straight into the swimming pool at the back of the house, the one that she'd only ever been in once before.

'You bastard.' Recognition hit just before she went under, she bobbed back up and he was standing at the edge. Laughing. And then he was in. Pressing her against the side of the pool with his hard body, his hand between her legs, fingers snaking under her shorts as his mouth came down on hers. His fingers pushed deep inside her body at the same time as his tongue thrust in her mouth. Hard, demanding and she had no place to go. And just when she thought she was going to come he pulled away. She clung onto the rail that ran along the inside of the pool, hanging on as he swung her legs up, dragged her shorts down and then lifted her ankles over his shoulders. His hair was sluiced down, dark against his scalp, the droplets of sweat replaced by the water from the pool, and the look of intent on his face was a pure aphrodisiac. His hands cradled her bum, squeezing her cheeks and then his mouth was between her legs, his tongue sweeping along her slit before he buried it inside her, flicked against her throbbing clit.

When he sucked she almost let go. His mouth was grasping, hungry forcing her sensitive nub into submission as the squeal escaped and she bucked her hips. She was gasping, twisting her body in his grasp and he just kept going. Sucking, flicking her with his tongue and then his finger snaked into her arse and she came. Came with an abrupt lurch that caught her unawares and made her see stars. As she shuddered he sucked, his mouth softer now, but just as demanding. Then he lowered her body down, but her feet never touched the floor. He lowered her just enough so that he could slide inside her. Fill her. He peeled her fingers from the bar, moving away from the edge so that she was clinging to him as he turned in the water as he forced himself harder into her. She clung, wrapping her legs around him, tightening as hard as she could so that she could feel every hard bit of him inside her. He took one nipple in his mouth, sucking until every nerve ending between breast and clit seemed to join up, on fire, and when he came she could feel it. The hot bursts of come bathed her inside as the cold water surrounded her outside.

'The smell of sweat.' He shook his head as though she was crazy, pulled her body from his and dumped her unceremoniously on the side of the pool. 'Did your mother never teach you not to disturb a man when he's working?'

'Nope.'

He pulled himself effortlessly out so that he was next to her.

'So, no shag in the stable then?'

'Cheeky cow.' And before she could object he gave her a gentle shove that sent her back into the pool and with a laugh headed back towards the stable block, dripping water in his wake.

By the time she got back up to the stables he'd taken his soggy jeans off and hung them over a stable door and was mucking out with just boots and boxers on. She had a horrible feeling her tongue was hanging out. 'Working up a sweat again for me?'

He laughed, his deep rumbling laugh. 'Always willing to work up a sweat for you, darling.'

'James?'

'Kezia?'

'Would you mind, I mean will you…'

'Go to the airport with you?' He smiled at her, and it was purely gentle because he cared. 'You couldn't stop me if you tried.' Which was what, deep down, she'd wanted to hear, but hadn't hoped to assume.

He put the fork in the barrow and stepped towards her, ruffling his fingers through her hair. 'I would have loved to have met your parents, Kez. I think they were pretty special people, with a pretty special daughter.' He brushed his lips over her eyelids. 'And I'm going to be there with you to welcome them back home.' He pulled her in close, held her tightly. And she didn't feel like crying, and she didn't feel scared.

They'd finished work then showered and changed before heading off to the airport in convoy with the undertaker's hearse. And they hardly spoken a word. She'd been hyped up in the morning, covering her nerves and he'd known and humoured her. And now he'd known just to be there. He was quiet on the drive back, letting her think. All that was left was the funeral and then she'd be on her own. But at least she had her plan and had some idea where she was going.

They were almost in the village before he spoke.

'I was thinking of going and seeing my parents. Letting them know what I'm doing.'

'Good.'

'Will you come with me?' He said it almost as an aside, but when she looked at his profile she could see how much it mattered. And it mattered to her too. To be asked.

'What if I'm not good enough for them?'

He laughed. 'I'm not looking for their approval, Kez. Though you're more than good enough for anyone.'

'I think Mum and Dad would be pleased I'm back here with

them.'

'I do too, pleased and proud of their spunky daughter.'

'Spunky? That sounds a bit cack.'

'Sparky? Or strange?'

She thumped his leg.

James gave a mock grunt of pain and turned the Land Rover into the riding school entrance. Being with Kez was a million miles away from being with Chloe. With Kez he felt like he'd come home and he wanted to give her whatever she wanted. She might not have changed him, but she'd dragged the passion he had inside out again, kicking and screaming. He didn't want to feel, but she hadn't given him a choice. 'The other guys will be back in a couple of weeks.' Which was a bummer, he was quite happy keeping her to himself. 'I don't want it to change anything.'

'Might put a downer on the shags in the swimming pool.' She grinned, gave him a cheeky wink, and then slid out of her side of the vehicle. He caught her just in time, pinned her against the side. Felt the familiar stirring in his body. 'And in the stable.'

'Guess we better cram as much in as we can in the next two weeks then.'

'Cram being the word.' She laughed, wriggling her breasts against his chest. 'I like being crammed by you.'

'I like cramming you.' And he didn't kiss her, he just rested his forehead against hers and let himself look into those green-brown eyes and knew that for a girl like this he'd surrender anything, even his soul.